Innocent VICTIM

written by
Karle Dickerson

digital cover illustration by
Michael Petty

To my mom and dad

Special thanks to:
Marjorie Gies, M.D.
Charmaine McLurkin, M.D.
Teens on Target, San Pedro, California

Second printing by Willowisp Press 1997.

Published by PAGES Publishing Group
801 94th Avenue North, St. Petersburg, Florida 33702

Printed in the United States of America

2 4 6 8 10 9 7 5 3

ISBN 0-87406-868-1

chapter

Pain makes men think.
Thought makes men wise.
Wisdom makes life endurable.

I read this proverb once on a fortune cookie that I got at a Chinese restaurant. I think about that proverb a lot, and I hope with all my heart that it's true. Sometimes I lie in bed in my room and smoosh up my eyes so that my floral wallpaper gets all weird. The pinks and greens sort of ooze into one another until it gets all greenish—like one big field. And before I know it, I'm back on the soccer field, unafraid, laughing, and running—the crowd in the stands is roaring like an ocean, "Shoot, shoot, SHOOT!"

"SHOOT, shoot!" Ms. Crownover, Hamilton High's soccer coach, yelled at me. Her kinky, red hair was flying as she galloped up and down the sidelines, her blue eyes boring a hole through me.

I took my eyes off the ball for one critical moment. Instead of considering that we only had seconds to win the game, I looked at my coach and considered just how much her red hair clashed with her purple uniform—big mistake. A green-shirted Cleveland High girl swooped past me, expertly controlling the ball, and my chance was lost. Gritting my teeth, I kicked into overdrive and swept by the girl just as she was about to clear the ball. I stuck out my foot and got lucky. It connected sideways and the ball shot to the right, flipping up chunks of mud. Lunging past her, I followed the ball, and even though Ms. Crownover was yelling, "Pass! Pass!", once again I found myself with the ball in front of the goal. Two golden opportunities in one minute! My pulse pounding in my ears, I positioned myself and WHAM! The way the ball rocketed into the goal was a thing of beauty. That poor goalie never had a chance! Her mouth flew open as the whistle blew. A goal, a point—the game! *How I love this game,* I thought wildly as the crowd went berserk in the stands.

"Hamilton! Hamilton!" Everyone was chanting.

"We won!" It was Caitlin Holmes, my best friend, who reached me first. Of course, she would. She was a forward and usually the closest to me on the field. She pounded my back and gave me a humongous hug. "Serious shot, J. T." Her face was flushed against her purple shirt, and her eyes sparkled. I was amazed that she didn't call me a ball-hog.

Looking back, I realized that I should have passed the ball to her, but that was how Caitlin was. She didn't get all tweaked about things like that. She was on my side no matter what I did. She was big on forgiving and forgetting, and that was one of the things I really liked about her. I was usually messing up, so her forgiving made things convenient for our friendship. Now her voice lowered. "Chase is here—and he saw everything."

I was gasping for air so loudly from all the running I'd done over the last hour, I wasn't sure I heard right. But I looked up over the swarm of purple jerseys headed toward me, and there on the sidelines, I caught an eyeful of Chase Phillips, major crush material. I didn't have time to get all weird just then because my teammates were swooping in, yelling, laughing, congratulating me, and going totally crazy because we had just won.

5

"State championship, here we come!" yelled Brooke Sherwood, our halfback.

"Good shot, Julia, but next time, don't hog the ball if Caitlin's wide open. And what's more, if you *do* keep it, don't let your eyes leave the ball for a nanosecond. It's not too often that you get second chances." That came from Ms. Crownover. But she was smiling and slapping me on the back, and I knew that she was just doing the coach thing and wasn't getting down on me. She was too jazzed herself. Our school hadn't beaten Cleveland High in soccer in years. We did our cheer and tried not to gloat as the green-shirted Cleveland High players gloomed their way off the field. I ran over to the goal and grabbed the game ball.

"Wow! Aren't you psyched? Chase came to watch you," Caitlin said as we started off the field. "I told you he was starting to notice you, but you wouldn't believe me. Believe it now."

My stomach was now doing high-impact aerobics, partly from our win and partly from the fact that Chase had come to see the game. And he'd seen me win! Suddenly, he was right next to me. I caught a whiff of some sort of lime cologne, and I got a full-on close-up of his incredible sea-green eyes. His dark brown hair was flopped forward. I wished I looked calm and pretty instead of worked up and sweaty. My face was probably as purple as my jersey. Clutching the ball, I looked sideways, past Chase's ear, while I tried to get a grip on myself. That had been hard to do lately around Chase Phillips. And that part annoyed me because I'd always prided myself on acting normal around guys, not massively idiotic like half the Hamilton High girls did.

"Good game, J.T.," Chase said to me. He grinned and his even, white teeth gleamed, mesmerizing me.

I'm totally in love with you, I wanted to say. Instead, I grunted. How was that for conversation with the guy of my dreams? I hardly had time to mentally kick myself before my one of my older twin brothers, Jeremy, shoved his way over to me. He jerked his chin at Chase, then glared at me.

"You bet it was a good game, but it's over," he said. "We've gotta go. I got stuck picking you up, and I need to be home like right now."

I looked to where Chase had been standing not a second ago, but he'd disappeared into the crowd. Turning, I glared at my brother. Who did he think he was anyway? I hadn't asked for a ride home in the first place, and now he'd completely blown my first real, face-to-face encounter with Chase Phillips. He and my other brother Jesse were starting to really

7

get on my nerves.

"Well, then go," I exploded. "I'll walk home."

Jeremy grinned at me carelessly. "No way, baby sister," he said just to infuriate me. "I was assigned to pick you up, and here I am. Now get a move on and change. I'll wait in the parking lot."

I shot Jeremy some daggers, then pushed past him toward the girls' locker room. My family was more than I could handle at times. I told Caitlin so as we showered and changed. Caitlin made noises like she understood, but no one, not even Caitlin—who's known me since we were babies together at Miss Attee's Daycare—understood my family. It was bad enough that my parents were massively over-protective of me. I mean, they make me wear a beeper wherever I go. But throw in twin senior brothers who've shadowed my every move since I came to Hamilton, and you have the recipe for insanity. Right now Jeremy was making me certifiable.

"He completely messed me over," I wailed to Caitlin as I stuffed my grimy uniform into my athletic bag and grabbed my backpack. "Chase won't come near me ever again. You should have seen how Jeremy looked at him. Like 'stay away.'"

"Don't worry," Caitlin said in her breezy

way. "You'll see Chase again around school to-morrow. He's bound to talk to you again. If it comes up, you can mention that Jeremy's harmless."

"I'm gonna get Jeremy," I vowed. I knew I wouldn't get much sympathy from Caitlin. She'd had a crush on my brothers since we were little, and she never thought they did anything wrong. I used to tease her and tell her that she'd started using me at Miss Attee's just to get a chance to hang around the double-Js. Trouble was, lately, she'd gotten pretty sensitive about it, so I'd stopped teasing. It was bad enough having a friend who had a crush. Try having a friend who has two crushes—on your brothers.

I slung my backpack over my shoulder and groaned under its weight. All of my textbooks were jammed in there. It was going to be complete Homework City for me tonight. Two tests and two study packets were due, and I really hadn't studied like I should have. Soccer practices and games had massively cut into my time.

"Well, at least you have two brothers who worry about you," Caitlin said. She hurriedly applied some lip gloss and mascara in front of the steamy locker room mirror, gave high-fives to two of our teammates, and then we

9

headed toward the door. "My brother couldn't care less. Can I snag a ride home with you?"

"Fine, but I don't see why we can't walk home without everyone getting in my face about it," I grumbled. "I mean, we live two blocks from school. What's the big deal?"

"*That's* the big deal," Caitlin said, her eyes flickering up toward the sidewalk by the parking lot, where a group of rough-looking kids huddled around a car. I'd seen some of them around school, but I never paid attention. I mean, Hamilton's so huge. If they didn't play sports, I really didn't know who they were.

As we drew closer, I could hear them laughing loudly and swearing. A couple of the guys were smoking, including one guy I knew of vaguely, Danny Lipofsky. Everyone called him "Wreck" for some reason. One of the girls, who was wearing a leather vest with no shirt under it, jumped up on the fender of someone's car and sat swinging her legs. Her thick boots made loud clumping noises against the tire.

"What a jerk," I muttered, but quietly. I didn't want anyone to hear. I didn't want any trouble. I'm kind of an expert at staying out of trouble.

Caitlin turned to me. "That reminds me,

did you hear that someone's nose got broken at the football game against Cleveland High two weeks ago?"

"Was he a good player?" I asked automatically. That was my worst fear—being injured and side-lined.

"It wasn't a player, and it wasn't a he. It was a she, and she was just a student in the stands. Some girls picked a fight with her, and she got pushed and broke her nose," Caitlin said. "I overheard someone talking about it after lunch."

I shook my head. I hadn't heard, and I didn't want to hear stuff like that. I mean, it happened to other people. My world had nothing to do with that kind of people. Anyway, much as Jeremy and Jesse bugged me, they were always there for me. Jeremy worked out and was big, so no one messed with him. Who cared about some stupid losers?

"The biggest problem those guys have is that they suck smoke and barf up black chunks of lung," I whispered to Caitlin, clutching my athletic bag tighter.

"No biggie," Caitlin said, her eyes darting around. "There are still tons of people around. Nothing could happen."

"I'm not worried about anything happening," I retorted. "I just think it's irritating.

And I think you worry way too much."

That was one of our main differences. Caitlin was a world-class worrier. She worried about everything. So worrying about a bunch of rough kids was right up her alley. Anyway, what Caitlin said was true. There were parents and coaches and students still leaving the game. No one would cause trouble right in the middle of a crowd like this. But then I thought of the football game Caitlin had just told me about. There had been tons of people around there, too. Probably a dozen people had seen someone break that girl's nose.

We walked by the kids sitting on the car, and I tried to keep my head up and look past them. *Look confident and walk with purpose.* Mrs. Crownover's words rang in my head. She'd taught us a unit on self-defense the first two weeks of school. Funny, now that I thought about it. It was like, "Welcome to Hamilton High. Now here's how to defend yourself."

"So this guy at this high school where my cousin goes got nailed for holding a piece," one of the guys leaning on the car said as we strode past. "They handcuffed him right in class and dragged him out."

One of the girls swore. "We'll have to be careful. We don't want to get nailed, too."

As we got nearer to Jeremy's car, I turned to Caitlin. "Piece? A gun?" She nodded. I shook my head. "Someone was carrying a gun in class?"

"I guess so," Caitlin said. "You heard it as well as I did."

"Weird, huh?"

"Yeah."

I was glad to open the door to Jeremy's car and slide in. It was enough to stress out about scoring soccer goals, doing mountains of homework, and getting Chase to notice me. I didn't have time to worry about people breaking each other's noses at football games and carrying guns with them to class.

"Can Caitlin have a ride home?" I asked Jeremy.

"Sure, Dork Breath," he said. He didn't have a chance anyway because Caitlin had already jumped into the car.

"Hi, Jeremy," Caitlin said in this high, lilting voice I couldn't stand that she used around my brothers.

But Jeremy didn't appear to notice. To him, Caitlin was just one of my dorky friends. At least that was how Jesse, my other brother, put it. Don't get me wrong. They were okay guys, but they were my brothers and since they were twins, there were two of them to gang up and bug me and put down my friends. I wished Caitlin would find someone else to get heart-tweaked over so I didn't have to deal with it at all. Caitlin tried to talk to Jeremy, but he just turned up the radio, and we sailed out of the parking lot, past the kids who were now leaning back on the hood of the car.

"They're going to totally cave in that hood," Jeremy said over the radio. "I'm glad it's not my car, or I'd have to inflict some damage on them."

"Oooh, tough guy," I said irritably. I hated when he acted all tough. It wasn't like him, and it seemed totally fake.

"You don't think I'd nail them?" he asked me, challenging me.

"Whatever," I said. "But speaking of nail, they were talking about someone who was nailed for carrying a gun to class."

Jeremy's eyes didn't leave the road. "Pretty stupid, if you ask me. You guys stay away from people like that."

"Du-uh!" Caitlin and I chorused at the same time.

"I mean it," Jeremy said.

There he was, giving me that big brother stuff again. Just because he and my other brother were seniors, they thought they had the right to watch over me like papa hawks. Like I couldn't beat up half of the wimps that walked around Hamilton anyway. Jeremy had been getting totally out of hand lately. I made a hideous face at him that he couldn't see and rolled my eyes at him. Like in a million years I'd ever get near people like that. I wasn't stupid.

"You know, when you really think about it, it is kind of scary around here," Caitlin said.

I could tell she was trying to keep a conversation rolling. We were driving past the Maxi-Mart, and I could see graffiti scrawled on the back wall. Then it occurred to me that Caitlin might be just trying to make small talk, but that didn't mean she wasn't right. We had lived here in Deer Springs, Oregon, forever, and for a long time, it seemed as if nothing ever changed. But somehow, in the last couple of years, stuff was beginning to happen. At first, it was just news stories about things happening downtown. But now there was graffiti on the grocery store where we went shopping all the time. And people were doing stuff at the high school we were playing against. Still, if you stayed out of the way of trouble, trouble would stay out of your way, I reasoned.

I asked Jeremy to turn on the heat. I didn't

like it that I had gone from being totally psyched about our win and the fact that Chase coming to the game to even thinking about guns and graffiti. It was a waste of time. I tried to switch the conversation back to the game.

"So did you see Cleveland's goalie?" I asked. "Her face completely fell off when I drove the ball into the net."

"Yeah," Caitlin said, smiling. She played with one of her silver earrings. "It was great. She had just started talking trash to me and said, 'Give it up. We've got this one, so why don't you just go cry somewhere?'"

"She said that?" I asked. Oh, sweet victory. I couldn't help hoping that the Cleveland players were crying on their bus all the way back to their school.

We talked about the game all the way home. It wasn't until I was in my room slouched over my homework that it occurred to me that I was thinking about guns and someone's nose being broken. Turning up my stereo loudly, I tried to drown out my thoughts. It wasn't like me to get all tweaked about things that didn't have anything to do with me. I wasn't going to start now.

Stupid, I thought as I flicked off my computer and crawled into bed that night after having stuffed my brains with geometry and history. I had better things to think about: soccer wins and Chase Phillips—and what I was going to say to him tomorrow.

chapter two

I am not a morning person. Let me repeat: I am *not* a morning person. So when the alarm went off the next morning, I did what I usually do—deny, delay, then finally, deal. Roughly translated, this meant that I let the alarm bzzzzt! as long as I could stand it, burrowed in bed with my eyes closed until my mom's voice cut through everything, then made my way to the shower without turning on the light. If I stumbled to the shower in the dark, I could put off for just a while longer the fact that it was time to dress for another day at school.

For some girls, like Caitlin, for instance, dressing was a huge project. For me, it was a slam dunk. One of my black skirts that all looked alike, and whatever shirt I could find that wasn't wadded up on the floor of my closet. The only decision was whether to wear the little silver soccer ball necklace I got one year for All-Stars or the tiny silver "#1" my grandpa gave me last spring before he died. Today I chose the "#1."

Of course, that was all before I remembered that Chase had come to see my game—and that meant he was noticing me. While he was in the zone, I figured, I'd probably better take another look at this dressing thing. Normally, I didn't worry too much about the fact that after a tough game my legs were covered with soccer bruises and scrapes. Today, it seemed like a good idea to check out the damage. I studied myself in the mirror. Chin-length, straight, brownish-blond hair. Your basic brown eyes. A small scar on my chin where I once took a soccer ball in the face. Those bruised legs! I departed from my black skirt and tried on another couple of outfits that covered my legs more. Ultimately, I decided it looked as if I was trying too hard and I ended up with what I'd started out wearing in the first place. Forget the bruises.

Then it was downstairs to grab the last of the good cereal before my brothers beat me to it. Turning on the radio full blast, I poured myself a mountain of Fruit Bombs.

"Good morning, Julia," my mom said, coming into the kitchen. She never calls me J.T. like my friends do. She always insists on calling me Julia. She smoothed the lapel of her navy suit, plunked her laptop computer and briefcase by the back door, and poured herself a cup of coffee.

"Hi, Mom," I said quickly between mouthfuls of cereal. My favorite song was playing, the one that always made me think of Chase, and I wanted to hear it.

"Could you turn down the radio?" she asked while she scanned the newspaper headlines.

"But, it's . . .," Seeing that mom-look she gave me—one that could burn a hole into a person—I sighed dramatically and did as she asked.

"I'm going into the office early so maybe I can catch your practice after school," she announced.

That came as no surprise. My mom and/or dad usually showed up at every game or practice that they could. My mom has been a classic soccer mom since the first time I suited up in a Totplay tournament. She even wears these dorky soccer earrings and what she calls her "good luck" soccer shoes. It was a given that at most games, I'd see my parents pacing up and down the sidelines. Of course, I'd long ago trained them not to shout instructions to me. It zaps my concentration. Anyway, I know more about the game these days than they do.

"Cool. See ya, Mom," I said taking one last mouthful of cereal. Dropping the bowl into the sink, I dashed out the door before she could tell me to ride to school with my brothers. At the corner, backpack in hand, I hung around until Caitlin came into view.

"Let's wait for your brothers. I'm, like, allergic to walking today." Those were the words she greeted me with when she finally arrived. Not "hi." Not "what's going on?" But "Let's wait for your brothers." Pu-leeze.

I shook my head. "Guess again," I muttered. "Let's walk." It was still too early. I was already wiped from my closet raid and was in no mood to watch the Caitlin flirtfest.

Caitlin shot me a pleading look, but I shrugged mercilessly, and we started off for Hamilton High. While we walked, I glanced over at her outfit, a pair of cocoa-colored flaring pants and a tight-fitting knit top. I had to admit they looked good on her. Of course, Caitlin's got these curves that won't quit, whereas I'm built like, well, a tree stump. Straight. A little thicker than I'd like to be. But strong, which was all that mattered, really. I smiled and walked a little faster to keep up with my best friend. We get so competitive sometimes, we can't even stand when one of us is walking faster than the other, let

21

alone when one out-plays the other in a soccer game.

"Do you realize that we have to win only one more game and we go to state tournament?" I asked.

Caitlin nodded and her shiny coppery hair danced in the sun. She kicked at an imaginary ball. "Do you realize that I've thought of nothing but that for months?" She stopped and held up her thumb and forefinger in the shape of a *J*. "Well, almost nothing else."

I didn't want to get into that. I didn't want to hear about how wonderful my brothers were. This crush of hers had been working my nerves since last summer before we started our freshman year at Hamilton High. But, of course, with their usual less-than-great timing, my brothers drove past me in their poor excuse for a car and honked. Caitlin lit up with a smile like a nuclear reactor in Stage Three. "Hey, Jesse. Hey, Jeremy."

Her smile faded as they drove past. "They didn't even stop. I knew I shouldn't have worn this outfit today. Too threatening."

I didn't tell her it had nothing to do with threatening cocoa-colored bellbottoms. It was because I'd shot them a don't-even-think-about-it look. But then I realized that Caitlin really was hurt, and I began to feel a blob of guilt. "Oh, it's not you—or your outfit," I said hurriedly. "It's because of me. I gave them the eyeball death threat."

"It bugs you that I like your brothers, doesn't it?" Caitlin said slowly.

It did. I mean, no one liked to see a friend in the grip of mad-guy disease. But I shrugged. "No, it doesn't bug me."

"Yeah, it does," Caitlin insisted. "It drives you berserko that I think they're cute."

"It's your business," I said evenly, examining a chipped nail to show how much I didn't care. But Caitlin's eyes continued to bore through me. I sighed and gave in. "Okay, so maybe I think it's a tiny bit weird. I mean, Guys Worth Liking should be cool and mysterious. You've known Jeremy and Jesse since they ran around in dinosaur jammies."

"True," Caitlin admitted. "But they sure don't run around in 'em these days."

There didn't seem to be any point in going on with this conversation, so I switched it to the group assignment we had for English. We were debating the pros and cons of open campus. The seniors were the only ones to have it, and a bunch of the underclassmen thought they should have it, too. Caitlin and I had to take opposite positions, so we argued cheerfully until we turned the corner at the front of our school—and stopped abruptly. Usually, right before school, the front lawn was half-empty. Oh, sure, there might be a few students sitting in little groups on the grassy knolls talking and laughing. But today it seemed as if the entire Hamilton High population was there—along with a bunch of police cars. And no one was laughing.

"Whoa, check it out. What's going on here?" Caitlin asked breathlessly.

"Wow. I don't know," I replied. I started counting police cars among the mass of students as we got closer. Our principal, Mr. Salazar, held up a bullhorn and started directing the students to stand back. One of the girls on our soccer team, Mia Sutherland, broke away from the group and came over to us.

"Can you believe it? Someone brought a gun to school today," she said, bursting with her news. "The cops are swarming all over the place."

"Unbelievable," I said. "Didn't I hear about someone else getting nailed for that just yesterday?"

Mia nodded. "Everybody's heard about that. Some guy named Gareth Weeks. He goes to Fairfield High. But someone brought one here today, and now they're doing a locker check."

"They can check all the lockers they want,

but they won't find it," I heard someone say behind me. I spun around to see who it was, but there were so many people surrounding me, I couldn't tell who'd spoken.

There it was. That feeling again. I didn't like it. I mean, one minute, we were discussing crushes and English assignments, and the next we were in the middle of one of those police-drama TV shows. It was one thing to have it on a TV screen. It was another to have it happening in real life. I shook my head.

"This is so stupid," Mia said.

I was about to say I agreed when she added, "I mean, who do the police think they are, snooping through people's lockers? Those are private property!"

I opened my mouth to say that I didn't care whose private property the police nosed into, I didn't want to be within twenty miles of a gun. But then I thought about the comment I'd just heard. It was clear that wherever that gun was hidden, it wasn't in a locker. So where was it then?

We were kept outside on the front lawn for about half an hour, then we were herded into the school gymnasium, where we had an unscheduled morning assembly.

"I wish we could find out what's going on.

They're just trying to keep us out of the way," Caitlin told me as we took our seats on the bleachers.

"Fine by me," I said, opening my notebook and pulling out my algebra homework. If this was like one of our usual assemblies, I could run through my homework and review my problems. I'd learned long ago how to grab odd moments to study.

After a while, I craned my neck to see if I could spot Chase on the bleachers anywhere, but no luck. The student body officers read the morning bulletin, including the news of our big soccer win. I soaked up the cheering as I scanned my homework and checked out again as a couple of teachers talked about nothing. Then we had to sing the school song. It struck me as kind of unreal. I mean, no one mentioned a word about what was going on in the halls of our school right that minute. We just sat there singing about how proud and grand Hamilton was and about honor and loyalty while policemen were searching our great alma mater for weapons. Then we sat there doing nothing for a while. Talk about bo-RING. Finally, we were released to go to our first class.

"Guess they didn't find anything," Caitlin said to me. There was only one police car left in the parking lot as we fanned out onto the campus.

I didn't know whether that was good news or bad news, whether it meant that the gun thing was a false alarm, or whether it simply meant that that gun was hidden where the police couldn't find it. I preferred to think it was a false alarm. By the time my history class was almost over, I'd convinced myself that the school officials had overreacted, like they usually do about things. And I could tell that most of my schoolmates thought so, too.

"It's not such a big deal. Mr. Salazar just made it into an event so he could get his name in the paper again," Tina Pratt said to me, taking her seat next to me in algebra class. She was one of those girls who dyed her hair with Kool-Aid. Today it was screaming green. She always dressed to look pretty tough. I generally hung out with the jocks, so I never bothered talking with her before. But suddenly, I realized she was the girl who'd been sitting on the hood of the car in the parking lot yesterday. I looked closer at her. She seemed to take that as a sign that I wanted to talk with her.

"And you know what else?" she added, her dark eyes big and luminous. "He must think that we're mentally impaired. Hiding guns in lockers. I don't think so. We know of way better places."

We? I looked closer at Tina. Nah, I thought. She didn't mean to say "we." She was just talking tough. My gaze slid to an ink tattoo she'd drawn on her ankle. It was a teardrop surrounded by little curlicues. Something made me ask, "So where *do* you hide guns?"

Tina regarded me, waited until Mr. Hennessy's back was turned at the board, then whispered. "You're a jock rah-rah. Why should I tell you?"

I shrugged. "No reason."

For some reason, she whispered, "Danny knows all the best places."

She was referring to Danny Lipofsky, who sat two rows over. The way she said it, it was like he was like the King of Cool or something. I knew for a fact that he was a blah. I stole a glance at him. He was the moody type. I used to wonder what his story was, why he was so quiet. He was on the JV basketball team. Not one of the stars, not as good a player as Chase, but adequate. Trouble was, he cut class and they were always threatening to drop him from the team if he didn't shape up. Why would he know good places to hide a gun? Tina, I decided, was just trying to talk big, like she knew something. She was probably just making it all up. I shook my head and tried to concentrate on algebraic equations. I wasn't a math loser, but algebra did give me problems. I needed to pay attention to Mr. Hennessy. Not to Tina and her talk.

All day long, there was an undercurrent of talk about—what else? Everyone at our lunch table was buzzing with talk of guns and blabbing about who it was who'd brought one. As for me, I kept looking out of the corner of my eye at Chase, who was eating with a couple of the guys on the JV basketball team. I was pretty sure he looked my way every so often, and once I thought he was smiling at me. Then again, maybe he wasn't smiling at me, exactly. Maybe it was that he was smiling at something someone said, but he happened to be looking up. Maybe Caitlin was right, and he'd talk to me. I'd waited for him to talk to me since September when I'd first realized how cute he was.

But as it turned out, Ms. Hoesche decided to spring a film on us, and it took all period. So I didn't get a single chance to talk to Chase. The film was still going when the bell rang, and he disappeared down the hall after class. *Oh, well,* I thought, elbowing my way through the crowded hallway after him. That was pretty much the way it had always worked with Chase so far this year. One minute, he'd seem interested. The next minute, nothing. At least everything seemed to be returning to situation normal again. I tried to put the "C" word out of my mind for the rest of the day.

Just before the end of sixth period, the PA crackled and Mr. Salazar announced that a safety assembly would be held at an undetermined date.

"Big whoop," I muttered as I fought my way to dump my extra books in my locker.

"This is all because of Lipofsky," I heard a girl I didn't know say to someone else by my locker.

"Is he the one with a gun?" I asked her. She looked like a senior. She might know what was going on.

"He doesn't have a gun. He just wants people to think that. It's just that he ticked off some group of tough guys 'cause he was cheating when they were rolling bones, and now they want to fight him," the girl said.

Her friend added, "He's going to get his face smashed, and now we're stuck going to a safety assembly." The two girls snorted in disgust and turned toward the stairwell and walked off.

Fights? Rolling bones? Smashing faces? I

shrugged and started toward the gym.

I was glad to escape to the familiar world of soccer practice. Out on the field, I could be with my teammates and forget everything. The field was my second home. As I ran, I became aware of every familiar dip and hill on the field. I knew where the slippery parts were, the places where a ball would skim neatly over the grass, as well as the places where a ball could die and be left wide open for someone to make a breakaway.

Running, I felt the air filling my lungs. Brooke passed me the ball, and I dribbled it, then looked at Ms. Crownover and passed it to Caitlin with a resounding "thwack!" Could she see that I was a kick-and-run goddess? I laughed at my image as I positioned myself.

All afternoon, I locked my eyes on the net, dribbled the ball up the field, and no one could stop me. Finally, Ms. Crownover blew her whistle and called us over after practice to talk with us about our next game. She gave me a couple of compliments, rare for her. As we walked toward the locker room, I felt light and floaty again.

Caitlin came up behind me and cut into my thoughts. "Geez. Ms. Crownover really worked our butts off today."

I smiled.

"Of course, you probably loved it," she said to me, shaking her head. "You never get tired." Her eye traveled over to the senior parking lot. "Hey, Jesse is over there. He's waving."

"Yawn! Not again," I said irritably, looking over at the sputtering blue chug-a-lug. Jesse continued to wave at me insistently. Couldn't I at least have a few feel-good moments before my brother started bugging me?

That's when I saw Chase standing by the fence. He lifted his chin at me. I froze. I mean, I didn't speak boyspeak. What did that mean? "Hi, I acknowledge your existence?" "Hi, come over here?" I hoped my brother hadn't seen him. Jesse would probably jump out of his car and scare him off like Jeremy did. I slicked back my sweaty bangs and wished desperately my face wasn't Perspiration City. Why couldn't this have happened when I looked halfway decent? I threw Caitlin a desperate look.

"Go see what he wants."

"What if he's just saying 'hi, no biggie'?" I yelped. "I can't just go over there."

"You have to," Caitlin hissed. "You don't want him to think you're blowing him off."

Caitlin was right. I sighed, smiled, and nodded to Chase. As usual, my heart started some epic pounding as I got closer to him. He was standing with his hands in his pockets with this sort of half-smile on his face. That lock of hair had fallen across his forehead again. I imagined myself pushing it back and the thought sent an electric shock through me.

"Hey," I said, hoping to sound casual.

"J.T.," he said, taking his hand out of his pocket and pushing back the stray lock.

Why couldn't I breathe? There didn't seem to be anything to say. I surfed my brain for anything—anything!—I could utter that would sound halfway nonidiotic. Zippo. Zero. Nada.

"What's going on?" he asked. "I saw part of your practice."

I nodded. Say something, say something. Where was the goddess of the field now? She'd disappeared completely and left a brainless wonder in her place. One who could only drink in Chase's sea-green eyes. One who was probably drooling. Unconsciously, I wiped my mouth. "Do you think there was a gun?" was the only thing that popped into my brain. Now why did I say that?

Chase raised his eyebrows.

"Forget it," I said in a rush. I couldn't believe what a dork I was.

"Yeah," he said quietly. "I know there was."

A shiver went through me. "I hate all this,"

33

I said. I was beginning to feel furious. After all, here I was finally connecting with the guy of my dreams and we were talking about guns. The last subject I wanted to talk about.

Chase nodded.

"Hey, Julia, move it." My brother's voice floated over toward us. I shot him a glare.

Chase looked over at him. "I'd better let you go," he said suddenly.

I shook my head while I thought of several painful ways to dispose of my brother.

"Ignore him," I said. "I've got time." I wanted to see what he was going to say next. He seemed like he was struggling to get something out.

Chase regarded me. "Okay. A couple of us were thinking of going to—"

"Julia, let's go!" Jesse yelled getting out of his car.

I looked unhappily at Chase.

"You'd better go," he said. "I'll talk with you later." He started off toward the field.

Tears of frustration filled my eyes, and I started off toward the locker room.

chapter

three

A FTER I told Caitlin what had happened, even she seemed annoyed at Jesse.

"I can't believe it," I wailed. "I just know Chase was leading up to something. Now I'll never know, thanks to Jesse."

"We've got to get him to wise up," Caitlin said. "I think maybe you're right—he's taking this big brother thing a little too seriously."

I didn't answer because I was so angry. Why couldn't Jesse mind his own business and get his own life, I raged silently. He and Jeremy seemed to have made it their life's mission to wreck mine.

"I'll handle this. Don't say a word to Jesse or I'll go postal," I hissed at Caitlin before I opened the car door.

"Not a word," Caitlin agreed.

We couldn't have said anything anyway because the car was filled with several of Jesse's basketball buddies—and Caitlin was too busy turning on her flirt machine. I tried to think about how I could get back at my brother, but a car full of noisy guys wasn't the best place to come up with a strategy. I had to sit there and watch my best friend make a fool of herself while my brother ignored her. It made me more angry. I sulked while we drove around dropping everyone off. Geez. Did Jesse think he drove a taxi?

After we dropped off Caitlin, I asked, "Where's Mom? She was supposed to come today."

Jesse muttered, "She called from the office and told me to pick you up. I saw you with that guy again."

"So what?" I snapped. "What's wrong with Chase?"

Jesse didn't answer until we got to our driveway. "Nothing's wrong with him. He's an okay guy. He's a decent ball player."

"Well, then, back off. I'll never get a chance with him if you barge in like Father Protector every time a guy comes near me."

Jeremy shook his head and shut off the ignition. He grabbed his basketball and some books and ruffled my hair. "You think you know so much."

I snorted, slammed the door to his car, and stalked to my room where I spent the evening playing "Always Yours" on my CD player over and over while doing my homework with a big, stupid smile on my face. In the privacy of my bedroom, it was easy to imagine that Chase had been about to ask me out. With just a little maneuvering, I could figure out a way around my brothers.

"Sorry I missed your practice," my mom said when I went downstairs to kiss her good-night. "One of our projects blew up at the last minute."

"No problem," I said, then turned to my dad, who was sitting at his desk going over some bills.

He took off his glasses, ran his hand through his thinning hair, and looked up at me. "Hi, baby." I winced. I hated the way he still saw me as a baby. I was taller than he was. And I could shred him on a soccer field. "You know, Jesse told me what happened today. You should appreciate the fact that he's looking out for you."

I snorted. "Well, I don't," I flashed. But something in Dad's face made me back off. I smiled weakly, like I didn't really mean it.

"Good. That's my girl." He returned to his work. I rolled my eyes and went up to bed.

The next day, I saw Chase a total of three times around school, but he made no move to talk to me.

"So I was right," I wailed to Caitlin after school as we changed into our soccer clothes. "Jesse ruined my life. I'm going to kill him."

"Don't," Caitlin said. "At least not until after he or Jeremy notices me."

I didn't add that in that case, I'd never get my chance. A person could lose her best friend saying things like that.

After school, during soccer practice, Brooke Sherwood seriously messed up her knee. I didn't even see how. One minute, she was running; the next minute, she was in total pain on the ground. The last I saw her, she was being loaded into her mom's minivan to be driven to the urgent care center.

"She'd better not be totaled. We need her for the finals," Mia Sutherland said grimly.

"I just hope she's okay," Caitlin, scowling at Mia. I could tell she thought Mia was scoring a zero on the compassion-o-meter.

Brooke showed up at school the next day wearing a brace and looking pale. "I can't play for a while," she announced. "The doctors aren't sure what I did to my knee. It's swollen."

"Oh, come on," I said impatiently. "Didn't they x-ray you or put you on some machine that could tell you what's wrong?"

"It wouldn't show on an X ray. It's probably

soft tissue damage," Brooke said. "But they're not sure."

"Oh, great," I muttered. I didn't want Caitlin to think I'd gone Mia-like on her, but I couldn't help it. We needed Brooke for this Friday's game against Wilson High. Alysha Johnson could play midfield in her place, but she didn't have Brooke's speed.

"We'll manage," Ms. Crownover told us at the next practice. I groaned as I watched Alysha lumber around on the field.

"We won't manage," I whispered to Caitlin while we dressed in the locker room after practice.

The next day, I'd just plunked myself in my seat for algebra when I heard two girls in front of me talking about some fight that had taken place before school.

"It was out by the maintenance shed," one girl said. "It was really gross. Blood everywhere."

The other girl's eyes widened. "Who was it?"

I didn't hear the name because just then people started streaming through the door. A few minutes later, Mr. Salazar's voice crackled over the PA. He told us that violence on campus wouldn't be tolerated, and that students caught fighting would face disciplinary action. Then he announced that a safety assembly would take place on Friday.

"A safety assembly?" Tina asked, sneering. "What a moron. Okay, so we have Sylvester the Safety clown come to sing to us, and that's supposed to stop people from settling scores? Come on."

I had to admit, she had something there. Anytime there had been any kind of problem at the elementary or middle school I'd attended, it seemed as if the next thing we knew, we were sandwiched into some sort of awareness assembly. They were always stupid—people singing and dancing about whatever subject it was. Then people just went on doing what they were doing in the first place. If people wanted to fight behind the maintenance shed and kill each other, they could go ahead, for all I cared. *Another safety assembly I can do without,* I thought as I doodled on my textbook cover.

Anyway, I had other problems. Nosy brothers and the Chase problem. And there was the problem with Brooke. We might be able to do without her for Wilson, but we couldn't manage to go much beyond that without her. We'd become such a team, the loss of any one person carried huge loser potential.

By Friday, Brooke's knee still didn't look

any better, and her doctor hadn't cleared her to play. I was depressed as we all filed into the auditorium for the safety assembly. First Brooke, now to have to listen to an hour of nothingness. At least I could sit with my friends. Still, I didn't want to be in a crowded gymnasium. I wanted to be out on the field right now, warming up and visualizing my play. Instead, I took my seat on the bleachers and waited.

Finally, Ms. Baker, the vice-principal, came on stage and tested the mike at the podium. She smiled and then got right to it.

"Did you know that guns are involved in one-quarter of all teenage deaths?" she thundered, gripping the mike and looking around at all of us.

I smooshed my eyes until she and her tailored suit were a blur of tan and navy. *More importantly, did you know that Chase's eyes are the color of a stormy ocean?* I murmured at her under my breath. Hmmm. Well, maybe it was more the color of a mountain stream. I still couldn't decide.

Bodily, I might have been in the safety assembly. But mentally, I was on Chasewatch. I swiveled back and forth, trying to figure out where he was sitting. After taking in a full dose of Chase sitting about three rows in front of me, my attention shifted back to the stage, where now a group of students was setting up chairs to look like a classroom. Several upperclassmen from the drama department began to do a role-playing exercise about confrontations.

Caitlin was sitting on one side of me. Partway through the role playing, Tina squeezed in on my other side.

"Hey," she said.

Caitlin looked her over and whispered to me, "Since when have you become buds with Tina Pratt?"

"Spare me," I whispered. "We're in math together. We're not buds—we've just been talking some lately."

For some reason, Caitlin's comment bothered me. Maybe it was just because I was annoyed in general about being forced to waste my time. I mean, it wasn't Sylvester the Safety Clown, but it was close. I was taking it out on Caitlin because I was sitting there watching an assembly that I didn't want to watch. None of this had anything to do with me. This was other people's problem. I closed my eyes and tried running through soccer plays. When I opened them, I saw that Tina was drawing designs in ink on her forearm.

"Do they really think people will stop

42

carrying pieces just because they do these idiotic assemblies and make us role play?" she
whispered.

I regarded her newest design, a small rose
crossed by a long knife, and asked, "What
would make people stop?"

She glanced at me, and I saw a small
flicker of surprise cross her face. "It's not that
easy," she said softly.

I sort of giggled because it seemed so silly.
"What does that mean on *my* planet?" I asked
impatiently. "It *could* be easy. Just stop, that's
all," I said. It seemed simple enough to me.

Tina gave me a look as if I'd just sprouted
an eye in the middle of my forehead, and she
started crossing out her drawing with bold,
slashing strokes. "How else are we supposed
to defend ourselves?"

Against what? I wondered as the role playing ended and Ms. Baker directed us to stand
up. "Stand up and look under your seat," she
said. "If you have a piece of paper with a
black *X* marked on the bottom of it, please
come up to the stage."

We stood up. Checking under my seat, I
saw that I didn't have an *X*, nor did Caitlin.
But Tina did. She yanked the paper free and
crumpled it up.

"I'm not going up there," she muttered as

she looked into a small mirror and drew a black *X* on her cheek.

I looked at the students filing up to the stage to see if Chase was among them, but he wasn't. So that was the end of my interest in the black *X*s. *How much longer is this thing going to go on anyway?* I wondered, checking my watch.

Ms. Baker told us to look around the auditorium at the empty chairs. She said each empty chair represented a gunshot victim. Finally, she dismissed us, and we filed out of the auditorium.

I was about to turn to Caitlin when Chase appeared at my elbow.

"Pretty intense, huh?" he said.

I nodded. I could feel my palms starting to sweat. Maybe now he'd tell me what he was going to tell me before my brother had interrupted. My eyes traveled over the expanse of the oversized green sweater he was wearing. He gave me a grin.

"So—" Chase began.

"Chase!" A tall, dark-haired girl swooped down on him, touching his sleeve. "I've been looking everywhere for you. We've just gotta talk about some stuff."

"Oh," Chase said, blinking at her, then at me. "Well, J.T., see ya around."

44

I watched them walk off. The girl walked so close to Chase that she might as well have jumped into one of his pockets.

"Did you see that?" I exploded all over Caitlin. "Who was that?"

Caitlin frowned and shifted her book bag. "That was Brianne Kelly. She's a sophomore."

"She's gorgeous. And she doesn't have bruises on her legs. All right, what do I do now?" I asked my best friend. I had had it. I didn't know how to deal with guys. I didn't understand what made them all eager to talk with you one minute, then walk off with willowy, non-bruised goddesses the next. Of course, when I really thought about, it wasn't like Caitlin would have any answers either. She'd never gone with a guy. Except for her experience with her crushes, she didn't have any guy know-how at all.

"Oh, never mind," I growled.

"I don't know," Caitlin. "Maybe it isn't as bad as it looks. You know you always get worked up before a big game. I'll think about it during my next class, and we'll discuss our plan at lunch."

"See? Jesse really did wreck it for me," I wailed just before we parted for our separate classes.

As I started toward my next class, I

45

became aware that everyone was completely crushing against me as they pushed past. It was worse than usual.

"What's your hurry?" I grumbled as I was slammed by a backpack.

"Fight," someone said in my ear.

Go figure, I thought. I mean, we'd just gotten out of an assembly on confrontations and all, and now everyone was getting all excited about another fight. A crowd was gathering by the stairwell. Craning my neck, I could see Danny standing in the middle of a bunch of students. Some guy I didn't know was facing off against him. I knew better than to watch. I pushed my way past and went into my class.

During the next class change, I saw Tina in the hall. Her eyes were bright, and her black *X* was still visible on her cheek.

"What happened?" someone asked her.

"Nothing yet," she whispered back, "but it's going to go down later today. Danny doesn't have to take this. I'm always telling him that, but he won't listen."

I hunched my shoulder, turned away from her, and opened my locker. I took out a couple of textbooks and returned to the important question about my situation with Chase. *Grim,* I decided. This Brianne Kelly, whoever she was, definitely had it over me in the looks department. I tried to console myself that maybe Chase really didn't like tall, dark, gorgeous goddess types, that really he preferred short, pale, stumpy types like me. Somehow, I had trouble convincing myself. The best thing Brianne had going for her was that she didn't have an interfering brother, I told Caitlin at lunch.

"I guess that's it," I muttered, staring darkly at my flattened ham-and-cheese sandwich. "I'm doomed. I hereby give up on Chase."

Caitlin gave me a lop-sided grin. "Like I believe you for a minute."

I glared and took a vicious bite of my sandwich. "I mean it," I snapped.

The minute I said it, I realized what a jerk I was being. I mean, Caitlin didn't deserve it. She was just as nervous as I was about the upcoming game and all. And there I went, snapping her head off. Her face got red, and without saying a word, she got up with her lunch bag and started to stomp off. I got up and tried to grab her arm, but she shook me off angrily.

"Fine," I said and slammed my sandwich into the nearest trash can.

At practice that afternoon, I was a mess. I

woofed several kicks, missed two great passes, and in general just stunk up the whole field. Caitlin shot me a look of disgust. I played even worse than Alysha, a thought that gave me absolutely no comfort.

When Ms. Crownover called the team over after our drills, she looked directly at me when she said, "Let me remind you that when we get to this level, the win goes to the team that wants it the most. Right now, it doesn't appear that this team wants it."

Mia glared at me, and I ducked my head. It was probably apparent to everyone how poorly I'd done. Caitlin was terminally annoyed with me. Ms. Crownover was annoyed with me. Chase seemed annoyed with me. I was annoyed with me.

"Hey, Jenkins," Ms. Crownover said to me, "whatever else is going on, keep your head in the game."

That is it, I decided that evening as I considered everything in the safety of my room. Chase was really messing with my head. I couldn't afford to be distracted now, not with state finals coming up. I'd worked too hard for too many years. I was incredibly lucky to be playing on the varsity team when I was only a freshman. I looked at the trophies and medals displayed on my bookshelf and at the autographed pictures I'd collected from players in the professional soccer league. I wanted to be one of them one day, and I'd never get there by woofing plays and blowing games.

So that meant one thing: I would have to put Chase out of my mind. Of course, this would mean I'd have to make some changes, like doing the detour thing on the route I'd so carefully worked out so that I'd be sure to see him. Filled with resolve, I went to my bulletin board and took down the yearbook picture of him I'd photocopied. Crumpling it up, I lobbed it into the trash can. Later, I called Caitlin and apologized for being a jerk. As usual, Caitlin forgave me right away.

The next morning as we walked to school, I told Caitlin about my newest plan. "I'm turning over a new leaf. I'm going to concentrate only on winning the state championship, so that means I've got to forget about Chase. I'm going to even give you my CD of 'Always Yours' to hide so I won't get tempted to play it all the time."

"I think this is drastic," Caitlin said.

"It has to be done," I said. "I'm wiping my mind of him."

Caitlin shrugged. "By the way, do you like my new nail polish job?" she asked. She stuck out her hand and showed me the bright purple and white tips of her fingers.

"Nice," I murmured. I couldn't get mad at her for changing the subject. Neither of us pays attention worth anything on game day.

Math class was terminally boring. Partly to stop my stomach from lurching at the thought of the big soccer game that day, I turned to Tina. "Did anything ever come of the fight?" I asked idly.

Tina shook her head. "Not yet. But something's going to happen soon."

"Like what?" I asked. I really didn't care, but like I said, I was bored, bored, bored.

"Dunno," Tina said.

"So what started it anyway?" I pressed.

Tina pursed her lips. "Oh, this loser started hassling Danny when they were rolling bones, and Danny didn't like it."

"So it was about the bones?" I asked, like I knew what bones were. I had meant to ask my brothers, but I'd forgotten.

"Yeah, about the bones. And then this guy *looked* at Danny."

"Ladies, take up your conversation after algebra, if you please," said Mr. Hennessy.

It was unbelievable. I figured with all the big whoop going on, the fight had to be something big. A look?

"Yeah," Tina whispered when Mr. Hennessy's

back was turned. "People shouldn't be looking at people if they don't want trouble."

It occurred to me that Tina seemed way more protective of Danny than most people would be. I wondered if she was crushing on him, the way I was crushing on Chase. No, I decided. Danny wasn't someone a person would crush on. Something about him scared me.

Before I knew it, it was game time. It was the last regular game before the first game of the state tournament. I suited up in my practice gear and stepped out onto the field. Sitting on the grass, I started my warm-up stretches. A couple of my teammates and I kicked the ball back and forth to each other until Ms. Crownover got there. *This is it,* I decided, watching a bunch of fans start to fill up the bleachers. Turning, I could see both of my brothers standing at the fence by the parking lot. I was actually glad to see them there today. I hoped my parents would get there soon. I'd show everyone, including Ms. Crownover, that Hamilton High's soccer team wanted the win.

Soon we were lined up facing Wilson's black-and-white shirted team for the kick-off. The game began. Seconds later I positioned myself for a pass, and the minute I had the ball, I exploded down the field, dribbling for all I was worth around a black-shirted player who tried to cut me off. As I ran, my lungs started to feel as if they were going to burst. *It's now or never,* I thought as I lined up my shot to the goal. My lungs were on fire.

"Push past the wall," I chanted to myself. "Stay directed."

This was it. Ready, aim. Suddenly I heard a popping noise by my left ear. In the next instant, I felt myself being lifted up in the air and thrown forward. Then I felt a searing pain tear through my forearm. I kicked the ball, but it didn't quite connect. My arm. It was in the way. It felt as if someone had ripped a red-hot wire through it. Clutching it, I looked down at the deep red liquid seeping through my fingers. *This isn't right,* I thought wildly before my world crashed into a sea of blackness.

chapter
four

LET me tell you, it was weird trying to play soccer in the dark. The spectators sounded seriously strange, like they were coming from far away. I tried to run, but someone had tied my shoelaces together or something and I couldn't move forward. If only my arm didn't get in the way so much. It seemed as if it was three times its usual size. Trying to cry out, I found I couldn't make a sound.

Then suddenly, the darkness exploded into bright, intense white light. My eyes peeled open. It took a minute before a man's blurry face floated in front of me. Did this guy know he wasn't supposed to be on the field? We were talking red card here. What was with him, anyway? Okay, so maybe he had these nice gray eyes that crinkled up at the corners.

"Don't move it," came a crisp voice. Was it

Ms. Crownover's? I opened my mouth to reply, but this whimper slid out instead. Out of the corner of my eye, I saw this plastic bag connected to a tube that was hooked into my arm. I closed my eyes and mumbled for my mom and drifted back toward the soccer game.

Those voices. Once more, they crept into my blackness. I felt myself being lifted and saw more uniforms leaning over me. I kept looking at the plastic bag hanging overhead. There were strangers' voices buzzing around me, saying things like, "Easy, now." "Let's see what we have here." "You're going to be all right." And then we pulled up to a building. Immediately, I was whisked in on a wheeled bed, and soon there were more faces leaning over me, a couple of them wearing green masks. I watched the green masks and wondered what was going on. Somewhere in the blur, I heard the words, "Drive-by gunshot victim." I wondered who they were talking about. Someone asked my name, address, and age. I tried to answer even though I didn't see the point. It didn't matter. Then someone asked me if I was allergic to anything, and I started to cry. Was I allergic to anything? I couldn't remember. I shook my head.

Right after that, two policemen leaned over me. I looked into their faces, but I couldn't tell what they were saying. They were asking me questions. "Who shot you?" "Can you tell us what happened?" I wanted to laugh, for some reason, but I couldn't make a sound.

"Where's my mom?" I tried to say. I wasn't sure if I actually said anything, but one of the faces said she'd be here soon, and then a green face stood over me and started talking some more. "Take her to X-ray."

I was wheeled in for X-rays, then somewhere in the blur, I heard something about being stablized and going in for surgery. Someone placed a mask over my nose and told me I was to count backward from ten. Then came blackness again.

Somewhere in the sea of sticky liquid I seemed to be swimming in, I eventually heard voices. I tried to swim toward them. I knew those voices. My mom's voice. My dad's.

"Mom," I croaked as I struggled to swim in the direction of the familiar sounds.

"Baby, I'm here." That was Mom's voice all right, but it was weird. I opened my eyes and peered up at her, but I couldn't see her too well. I tried to move to get away from the heavy thing on my arm. Big mistake.

"Owww!" I howled. "This thucks!"

"Julia," my mom said sternly. That was better. That sounded more like her. The sticky liquid began to release its hold on me.

"Well, it duth," I said, even though my tongue stuck to the roof of my mouth. "My arm hurtth."

"I know it does," my dad said.

When I turned to look at him, my eyes began to focus. Then it registered. I wasn't on a soccer field. I was in a green room with lights around me. I was in a hospital. Then I remembered the pain in my arm I had felt just when I was about to kick the ball. Something had happened to my arm.

"I broke it, didn't I?" I gasped between spasms of pain. I mean, I'd broken my arm once before when I was seven and had trashed my bike on our steep driveway. Thing is, I don't remember it hurting this bad.

I saw my mom look at my dad, and I don't know why, but I got scared all of a sudden. Real scared. I tried to sit up.

"I'm going to die?" I squeaked.

Instantly, they were all over me. "No, no, don't move. You're not going to die. Nothing like that," Dad said in a rush.

Dr. Gray Eyes in the green scrubs pressed me back. "You're going to have to hold absolutely still."

"I am in the hothpital, aren't I?" I said wildly. I mean, the hospital was where Grandpa Pete had gone to die. People went to

56

hospitals to die. I was going to die, too.

Mom and Dad leaned over me. "No, you are not going to die," my mother said loudly and firmly, like I'd just done something wrong and had gotten caught big-time. "Now you stop talking that way."

I stopped talking that way. You don't mess with my mom. Anyway, my arm was hurting like crazy again. For a few seconds, I thought maybe dying would be okay if it would make me stop hurting. The last thing I remembered seeing was a green mask coming at me with a needle.

"I don't like nee—" I mumbled, then I slept.

When I woke up, it was dark outside. I was in a room and it was bathed in an eerie glow of lights. There were machines and dials all around me. I studied one machine that had a weird bleeping light and I wondered what it was for. But then I realized my lips were on fire, and I tried to lick them, but my tongue stuck.

"Auuu," I cried out. Even in my fuzzy world, I felt kind of embarrassed. Why didn't my mouth work? It had something to do with my arm. I turned my head to look at my arm. It was covered with a cast.

"Are you awake?" a voice said. "I'm going to turn on the light just a little."

A green-masked face swam before me, but even though it was swimming, I could see that it was a woman's face. The eyes were deep blue and they looked nice. The woman gave me some ice chips on a plastic spoon. I sucked them and the melted ice trickled down my throat.

"What's wrong with my arm?" I asked slowly and turned to look at the cast. My arm had to be under there somewhere. I couldn't find it, so I went back to sleep.

I woke up again, and this time it was light outside. My mom was sitting there in a chair with her eyes closed.

"Hi," I croaked. "I need water."

My mom leaned over me. "Here you go," she said, holding a cup for me with a flexible straw sticking out of it.

I sipped, then stopped as a giant wave of pain swept over me.

"Ohhh," I wailed as the wave got bigger and bigger until I couldn't even breathe.

"Do you need more painkiller?" my mom asked.

I nodded, and she pressed a buzzer thingy by my bed. A nurse came into the room and studied my chart for a moment. "I'll be back," she said.

The nurse gave me some pills, which I

took, and a couple of minutes later, the pain wave passed. I sat there for a moment, enjoying the pain-free experience. I mean, you don't think about pain normally, until you have it big-time. But then I made the mistake of jerking the IV just a teeny bit.

"This s—," I started to say.

"Don't say it," my mom said automatically.

"I don't get it," I said, after the newest pain blast settled down. "I'm sitting here in a hospital and all you care about it is my language."

My mom rubbed her eyes, then managed a sideways grin. "I know. I guess it's, well, it's because I know how to handle bad language." She looked at me for a moment. "But I don't know how to handle you lying here in a hospital bed because you've been shot."

The words hit me, and I blinked a few times. "Shot?"

My mom nodded and started to cry.

"Shot?"

My mom nodded again. "Gunshot. Someone in a car drove by the soccer field and shot you," she said.

Just like that. I, Julia Jenkins, had been shot. Yeah, right, I thought, wondering for a sec if my mom had weirded out on me, saying something like, "Oh, by the way, Julia, you were shot." But as my mind cleared some, it all made sense. I mean, this whole business lately about guns being brought to school. Did I really think whoever brought them just brought them without intending to use them? Okay, so why did "whoever" use a gun on me? I looked at my arm. My eyes traveled over the cast. At the end of everything, I could see my hand, which was sticking out. Well, I still had an arm and my hand anyway. A zillion questions jumbled around in my head, but none of them squeezed out. I closed my eyes, half-afraid that the pain would come back and overpower me again if I breathed.

Finally, I asked one question: "Where's Dad?"

My mom smoothed her rumpled jacket. "He stayed here all afternoon and evening. But after the doctor told us that you'd be okay, I told him to go home and rest. He went home to get some sleep."

"Oh," I said. Well, the doctor said I'd be okay. Good. I guessed that meant I'd get up and go finish my game. But right now I wanted some sleep. And I wanted to figure out why someone wanted to shoot me.

The next day was a blur of pain blasts and medication. Every time I woke up, some green-masked medical types were jabbing me with needles. Once a policeman came in my room, but I didn't understand what he was saying. I just kind of kept looking at his fat fingers and thinking that they looked like sausages. I think I said I didn't know anything, so he left. This was fine with me because I wanted to sleep, and I wanted to escape the white-hot burning in my arm.

The next morning, after the doctor had been by, the nurse announced that they were moving me to another room. Whatever that meant.

"This is good news," my mom told me as they wheeled my bed down a long hallway. "They're going to let us take you home soon, and you'll be starting physical therapy and be on your way to recovery."

"Cool," I said, wincing as the bed hit some sort of bump in the hall. I eyed the drip tube hooked up to my arm.

The next time I woke up, I saw that my room had a window. I kind of liked that. I also saw that I had gotten a whole load of flowers. Sometime during the day, someone brought in a giant teddy beat with a get-well card signed by everyone on my soccer team. For some reason, it made me cry.

I cried again when my dad and my brothers came that night. Partly because my arm still hurt like crazy, and partly because I guess the whole thing was sinking in: I had been shot and I didn't know why. Suddenly, I felt anger creeping up on me. It wasn't fair. I had never hurt anyone. But someone *had* hurt me.

"Hey, Dork Breath," Jesse said, leaning over me.

Normally when he said that, it made me want to punch him out. Right now, however, it didn't make me mad. My brother's height was comforting somehow. I grinned, but as I did so, I felt my chapped lips crack. Jesse held my other hand and asked me how I felt. I rolled my eyes.

"Who did it?" Jeremy asked, standing by my head.

I blinked at him. Like I knew?

"I don't know," I answered. The police had asked me that, and I'd given the officers the same answer.

Jeremy's fist clenched and unclenched. "We'll find whoever shot you."

"So what happened anyway?" I asked.

My mom pursed her lips. "It all happened so fast. We were watching you running with the ball and the next minute, we heard a crack, and you were down on the field."

"At first everyone thought maybe you'd just tripped or something," my dad added.

"But you were bleeding, and people started

screaming and ducking. The police think you were shot by someone from a car driving by, but there was a lot of traffic on the road at that time, and no one saw anything," Mom continued.

Jesse squeezed my hand. "Any ideas?"

"The police asked me that," I said. "I don't know. I wasn't exactly looking out on the street to see if anyone with a gun was going to point it at me. I mean, I was playing a game."

I looked down at my feet and pulled them out from under the light blanket. Something made me wiggle my toes. My feet were okay. I could still play. "So did we win?" I asked.

My mom shook her head and made a weird noise. Was she laughing? Suddenly, I was angry.

"It's not funny," I yelled.

"I know, I know," my mom said.

I could see the tiredness in her eyes. And that reminded me that I was tired. I was vaguely aware that someone came in and told my family that visiting hours were almost over. But even though I was sleepy, I felt afraid when my brothers left. Since we didn't know who shot me, how did I know that someone might not try to shoot me again? Could they come into the hospital and finish the job? I wondered if I could wedge a chair against the door to keep whomever out, but then a wave of sleepiness swept over me, and I drifted off into darkness.

chapter
five

"HEY, J.T. Cool hospital gown. Very fash-ion-forward."

Caitlin sailed into my room the next day, carrying another teddy bear wearing a soccer jersey and plunked it on my bed. I glanced down at my gown, taking care not to move the tubes attached to my hand too much, and snuggled the bear next to me.

"Thanks," I said, not wanting to show how glad I was to see her. "I had my personal shopper send it over from The Fashion Zone."

"I'm jealous," Caitlin joked. Then she said, "Now let me me see your arm," and walked over for inspection. She shuddered, looking quickly at me to see if I'd noticed.

"I know," I said, shifting uncomfortably. "Gross, huh? And I guess there's some metal plates and stuff under that."

She sighed and sat down at the end of my

bed. "Well, actually, there's nothing to see since they've got it all covered up with your cast."

I winced. "My arm's under there, all right. It reminds me all the time."

Her eyes grew soft. "It hurts a lot, huh?"

I shrugged with my right shoulder, not daring to move my left shoulder. The pain-killers were working right now, and I didn't want to mess with it. But just then, a woman wearing a paper thing that looked like a shower cap came in and told me it would be a good time to take my blood. I wanted to tell her that I could think of a better time, but I didn't. She looked totally cranky. I held up my other arm. I rolled my eyes at Caitlin as the Grinch poked me with the needle.

"Can I please tell you how much fun this is not?" I said with a scowl after the woman had left with my blood sample.

"I hate blood tests," Caitlin said, shivering.

"I don't exactly love them myself," I muttered. "I'm just glad I was out of it when they operated on me. I don't think I'd have wanted to know beforehand they were going to go in and rearrange a bunch of pieces in my arm."

Caitlin's face smooshed together—she was that grossed out. "Your mom told my mom that they operated on you for, like, almost two hours."

"That's what I hear," I said, nodding my head. "I was totally out of it, so I didn't really clock the doctor." But then I didn't feel like joking anymore. "They showed me the bullet. It was a nine-millimeter, if you want to know. I guess that's the gun of choice these days. They said I was lucky my radius was broken cleanly so they could put my bones together and not have to go to a bone bank, whatever that is. It's better if they can use your own bones. I don't know why. I didn't ask."

"So does your arm still work?" Caitlin asked.

"I think so, but I haven't really wanted to test it. I'm supposed to keep it still. I guess I was lucky that it missed some nerves and all. And I'm lucky it's not my right arm."

Caitlin sucked in her lips, then blew out her bangs. "So how's the food here?"

"Your basic non-edible gak. Now I know where Hamilton sends its leftover cafeteria food."

Caitlin looked around my room. She got up and read the cards on my flowers, then turned around. "This is so weird. I can't believe I'm here visiting you because you were shot."

"I can't believe it either," I said. "But I get outta here tomorrow, and the med types say I'll have to hang out in bed at home to recover for a while, but, hey—at least it's not my leg."

"Well, you won't be able to play soccer for a while, that's for sure."

I scowled. "Tell me something I don't know."

Caitlin gave me a long look. "What are we gonna do without you?" she asked.

For some reason that irritated me. It was like I was dead or something. "Well, it's not like I won't be around, so 'without you' isn't exactly the way to put it."

Caitlin tossed back her bangs. "I didn't mean it like that," she said and then paused. "They called the game, you know. So we'll have a rematch next week. But we're toast without you. No one else can score."

I turned toward the wall for a moment. I didn't want to act like the team couldn't do it without me, but I knew there was probably no way we'd ever get to state now.

"I feel so guilty," Caitlin. "I mean, it could have been any of us who got shot. It doesn't make sense that it was you."

"None of this makes sense," I almost whispered.

"I brought this," Caitlin said, unfolding a scrap of newspaper and thrusting it toward me.

It was an article about the shooting. "Hamilton Student Shot at Soccer Game." In smaller type under the headline were the words "Police have no leads." Then I saw the photo.

"That's my eighth-grade school picture," I wailed. I hated that picture. I looked like a geek in it. My eyes traveled down to the words below, but they blurred before me.

"I want to know who shot me," I said in a low voice as I handed the article back to Caitlin.

"It's totally buggin' out everyone at school," Caitlin said. "No one talks about anything else. They've got these special crisis counselors the kids can go see if they want. Some of the kids are going."

"Oh," I said. I didn't know what else to say.

Caitlin looked at the floor. "I'm so sick of answering questions. Everyone thinks that since you're my best friend that I should know everything. The police came and interviewed a couple of people. They asked me some stuff. They're offering a reward for anyone with information. But no one saw anything. No one's got a clue."

I digested this for a minute. Whenever stuff happened, people around school usually knew what was going on. The fact that they didn't was weird with a capital W. Of course, maybe someone knew but didn't want to clue in the police.

Then I had to ask. "Have you seen Chase around?"

Caitlin nodded. "Yeah. He called me up last night. I didn't even know he knew my number. He asked for the report on you—and he said he saw your picture in the paper."

I sank back in my pillow, a smile creeping over my face. That was good news anyway. But then I wrinkled my nose as I thought about the fact that he'd seen my picture.

"There's something else I should tell you," Caitlin added. "Danny hasn't been at school for a couple of days now and people are saying he did it."

I considered that for a moment. I mean, Tina had hinted that he'd brought a gun to school. But then again, I kind of got the idea that more than one person was carrying one. It could be anyone.

"Danny," I said with a snort. "Not possible. I mean, he plays on the JV basketball team and all. People with guns are, like, you know, total criminal types. Know what I mean? The guys who look wild-eyed and scary and hold up convenience stores. It's got to be gang members or someone from another school. Like some really out-there bad person type."

"Danny doesn't have the best rep around," Caitlin said.

"No way. Not Danny," I said firmly.

"Well, I'm just telling you what people are saying, that's all," Caitlin tossed her head. "And another thing. Mr. Salazar is starting to blab about zero-tolerance and stuff. We're not allowed to carry back packs anymore, unless they're clear. Now Mr. Salazar is talking about taking away open campus privileges for the seniors."

"Great. Now the seniors will be mad at me," I said. I didn't see what open campus had to do with anything anyway.

Caitlin looked away. "They know it's not your fault," she said. "You know, your brothers are outta their minds about what happened to you."

"I can't come to school for a while," I told Caitlin. "I guess I'm going to have a tutor or something so I don't get behind and flunk out of everything."

Caitlin chewed her fingernail and asked if I knew how long I'd be out of school. I said I wasn't sure. It depended upon my recovery.

My arm started aching, and some nurse came in to tell Caitlin she'd have to go.

After Caitlin left, I stared out the window, not really seeing anything. I thought about Chase for a while and wondered what it meant that he was getting reports about me.

That had to be good, right? Like he cared or something. But then I began thinking that maybe it was just curiosity. I mean, if some girl were shot at our school, I'd want to know about how she was doing, even if I didn't like the person. Anyway, he was probably a lot more interested in Brianne Kelly. She wasn't wearing a backless hospital gown. She didn't have metal plates and pins in her. No, she was probably wrapping two very healthy arms around him.

My arm started to do a major pain dance about then, and my thoughts turned to Danny. Was it true? Could he have shot me? But I kept coming back to the same place: Confusion City.

Later that afternoon, a woman came into my room. She was tall and thin and she told me her name was Mrs. Anderson, and that she was a social worker. She asked me how I was doing and if I wanted to talk about anything. The way she kept looking at me—did she think I was crazy or something? I told her I didn't want to talk, but she hung out in a chair in my room anyway and asked me about school and dreams and other stuff. I was glad when she left. I mean, I had told her I didn't want to talk. Later, one of the doctors told me that after traumatic experiences like

I had, they send in social workers to try to help. I didn't say what I was thinking—that I didn't see why everyone thought it helped to talk. Even thinking about what happened made me feel worse. I just wanted to forget about it, not blabber about it forever.

Ms. Crownover came the next day during visiting hours. She was wearing a dark blue dress. It was weird seeing her dressed up instead of in her usual athletic sweats. Even her crinkly hair was slicked back at attention. She looked uncomfortable and she paced my room while she talked to me about a bunch of nothing. She didn't mention soccer at all, other than to say everyone on the team missed me. I got that feeling again, like I'd died and I was the last one to know it. I was kind of relieved when she left.

My mom and dad came as usual the next day, but this time the police came with them. One of the policemen, an older guy with a thick brow that traveled all the way across his forehead, had me go through last year's yearbook pictures and some others they'd brought. It was no good. I mean, I was out playing soccer, not looking around to see who might shoot me. I kept telling people that, but no one listened. They were all sure I knew something I wasn't telling.

The younger guy asked me about Danny, but all I could tell him was that Danny played on the JV team, and that he wasn't really all that good. I didn't mention the gun thing, because I didn't know for sure. All I knew was what Tina had told me, and it had occurred to me that Tina wasn't always one for the truth. The police seemed annoyed with me when they left, which was stupid because if I had known anything, believe me, I would have told them.

"Only a couple more days, and you'll be coming home," Dad said, leaning over to ruffle my hair. "Though I know you'll miss this place."

I rolled my eyes, but after everyone had left, I realized that the idea of going home wasn't as comforting at it seemed.

The night before I was released from the hospital, I started getting scared. It wasn't like being in the hospital was fun or anything, but it did feel safe. The one time I made my way down the hall toward the front desk, I'd seen a uniformed officer standing guard by the door. I got the feeling that I was secure here. Something told me that I'd never feel this safe again at home. I couldn't sleep at all that night. I lay awake in the darkness listening. I wasn't sure what I was listening for.

Sunshine was streaming in through the window when I woke up the next morning. Everyone seemed to be talkative, including the volunteer lady who came in to bring me breakfast. She saw the flowers from my soccer team.

"I heard about your team," she said cheerily. "It's the winningest girls' team Hamilton's had in a while."

I tried to smile. She showed me pictures of her daughter, who, it turns out, went to Hamilton, too. She was a junior and I didn't know her, but I told the lady that she looked nice and all.

"It's horrible what's going on over at that place," the lady said, glancing at my arm. "Darcy's afraid to go to school."

Tell me about it, I thought. Actually, I was glad that I wasn't going back for a while, that a tutor would be coming to my house.

Then someone named Doctor Reynolds came in. He checked me over and asked if the painkiller they were giving me made me sick to my stomach or anything. I shook my head, and he gave me an odd look, then said, "You keep away from rough kids."

As if I hung around them! I sat up in bed and got ready to protest, but all of the sudden my arm started to hurt again, and I sucked in my breath instead. Dr. Reynolds turned back to his charts and told me I'd be cleared to go home by late morning.

About an hour later, my dad and Jeremy came to pick me up.

"Where's Mom?" I asked.

"She's getting your bedroom ready," Dad said as he and Jeremy gathered up all my stuff.

After I was checked out, I was wheeled out in a wheelchair. Don't ask me why. It wasn't like I'd hurt my leg or anything. I was gently loaded into my family's minivan. Every bit of movement set my arm throbbing and took my breath away. Finally, I was settled in the backseat with a blanket tucked around me.

No one talked for a while as we set out, and for some reason, that bugged me.

"So what's been going on since I've been gone?" I asked, trying to make conversation. I had only been in the hospital a few days, but it seemed like a million years. As we drove along, I kept looking out the window at the buildings we passed. I don't know why, but I guess I kept expecting things to change. I mean, in a couple of seconds, my whole life had changed. So it made sense that things around me would have changed, too. The weird thing was that everything was the same. Only I was different.

As we passed the grocery store, Jeremy turned around and said, "You okay?"

I nodded, but Jeremy's eyes didn't leave my face for a few more seconds.

There didn't seem to be anything to say. I was too tired to think anyway. It was weird, but the whole deal of being checked out of the hospital had totally worn me out. I was glad when we pulled up in front of our house. I allowed myself to be lead to my room, where my mom fussed around my bed for a while, and I slept.

I did a lot of sleeping those first few days home. Even when I was awake, I didn't feel like I was really awake. For one thing, I was filled up with medication. For another, when I wasn't fuzzy because of the medication, I was dealing with the pain. It was almost like my arm became the enemy. It was like we were forced to be roommates, me and my arm. I would glare at my arm when it hurt, and it throbbed back, daring me to move it even slightly. Sometimes, for no reason, I would burst into tears, and my mom would come into my room and stroke my hair and tell me everything would be okay. She'd help me to the bathroom and back to bed again.

"I'm so sorry this happened to you," she'd

say over and over.

My dad would say the same things and my brothers didn't talk much at all. They'd just hang with me and try to tell me stupid jokes. I didn't get them, but I'd stop crying and try to smile. After a while, I'd drift off back to sleep.

One afternoon, my mom came into my room with this bouncy young woman named Lisa. She said she was a physical therapist and that we were going to start to do some exercises. We really didn't do much, just a slow, stretching exercise or two and some leg lifts, but still my arm hurt like crazy. I took a couple of pain pills and went back to bed. I wasn't sure if it was real or a dream, but all of a sudden, Chase appeared in my bedroom door with Jesse. I couldn't be sure, but I thought I said hi and I kind of wondered if my hair looked horrible. Chase stood there for a while, then just before he left, I think he kissed me on the forehead. I wasn't sure about that either. I didn't want to ask because I didn't want to hear that maybe it was all a dream. For a long time after that, I dreamed shapeless dreams.

Soon my dreams became stronger and stronger, and sometimes I'd wake up in the middle of the night, listening to the sound of my breathing and waiting for my arm to start hurting. And then I'd feel this awful black fear start to creep up on me. It got bigger and bigger until I felt like screaming. I'd try to think through soccer plays to try to blot out the fear, but I was starting to forget them. And that scared me, too.

Soon, I started to have a stream of visitors. First, it was a couple of family friends. Then after that, it was Caitlin with a couple of my soccer teammates. Mia and Brooke sat on my bed and peered at my cast and asked me a zillion questions.

"So does it hurt?"

"Did you see who did it?"

"Did you hear we won the game against Pacific Ridge?"

I tried to answer them. Yes, it hurt, thank you very much. No, I didn't see who shot me. Yeah, I'd heard we'd won the game, barely. I answered a few questions that no one asked me. Yeah, I'd cried when I found out the team had won the game without me. Yeah, I would have cried if we'd lost. Yeah, I cried a lot for no reason. And yeah, I was scared. Scared of getting shot again. Scared of being this angry and sad forever. Scared of being stuck in my room forever while the world whirled on without me.

chapter

six

SINCE kindergarten, I have never missed more than a day or two each school year because of sickness. But whenever I did stay home, I kind of liked it. Okay, so I missed my friends and all, but I'd blast my CD player, read comic books, or do whatever. Of course, I liked getting back to school, but it was kind of cool to take a day or so out to do the sniffle thing.

But staying in bed day after day because I'd been nailed by a bullet was a whole different thing. For one thing, I never knew when I'd be totally swamped by the pain. I mean, one minute I'd be just cruisin' along, and the next I'd be sweating and clutching my arm. It was like anytime I started to feel better, someone would yank a chain that was connected to my arm. I'd take my painkillers and wait for them to kick in and wonder when the next pain blast would come.

There was another problem. Even though my teachers were sending home my home-work assignments, and this grouchy old tutor named Mr. MacPherson came over almost every day, I had plenty of time to do nothing. I was way beyond bored. I mean, pu-leeze. How many hours of TV can people watch before they get all whacked out? I know there are people who can't imagine life without the tube. They're the type who like infomercials and reruns of really old sitcoms, never mind shopping via TV. But count me out. My eyes were totally rolling in my head before the first batch of commercials. Even watching the sports channel (Jesse's idea) didn't help. I mean, I wanted to be out there playing, not watching other people run around doing things I used to do.

And there was one more problem. I'd worked for years conditioning myself so I wouldn't go panting around the soccer field. You know, running with my dad, doing these weight ex-ercises in our basement with my brothers to strengthen my legs, and stuff. I'd gone to a zillion practices and listened to a zillion coaches telling me to do more push-ups and things to buff up. I had posters all over my room that said things like, "Each step taken today is an investment in tomorrow's strength." And now, right in front of my eyes, even with the physical therapy exercises I was doing, my legs were totally doing a flab spiral. And so were my arms, for that matter. So what was going to happen when I finally got my arm back and went out on the soccer field again? Was I going to get out there and then totally wimp out because my muscles had done a disappearing act? I'd be like those duck-and-scream sports girls I couldn't stand.

"It's not fair!" I whimpered to Jeremy one afternoon as he came into my room, carrying a load of homework he'd brought for me from school and dribbling a teeny basketball. He dropped the books on my bed and shot the ball into my laundry basket.

"Life's not fair," he said, then scooped out the b-ball and tossed it gently in the direction of my good hand. "Homework isn't fair."

"You're so-o-o-o sympathetic," I said sarcastically as I caught it and heaved it back at him with my right arm. Big mistake. It joggled my left arm and sent up an alarm to my brain. "Bzzt. Movement. Punish the unit. Send out the pain signals."

Jesse sat backward in my desk chair, his long legs splayed out in front of him. He was wearing this seriously grotty gray college

T-shirt. Now that he was applying to colleges, he was beginning to look like a walking billboard for different universities.

"Raiding the college bookstore T-shirt section again?" I said as soon as I'd stuffed the pain back where it came from.

Jesse grinned. "Nope. A girlfriend gave it to me," he said.

"That's just because she's applying there, and she wants you to go there, too," I said to get back at him for his sympathy shortage.

Jesse blushed. "I think not, little sister."

I wiggled my eyebrows to show that I didn't believe him, then to my embarrassment, I felt my eyes well up with tears. I was turning into a regular crying machine these days.

"Are you bummed because life isn't fair?" Jesse asked gently.

I was, but I shook my head. I mean, how could I describe how afraid I was about him and Jeremy leaving for college—and leaving me alone here?

"No," I said. "I'm bummed because you're going to be leaving for college. You and Jeremy."

"It's not for a long while yet," Jesse said. "And unless our SAT scores come in okay, it might not be at all. If you really want to know, I think I choked, and I'll bet Jeremy's scores weren't much better. It took us forever to figure out how to do our applications on that software the colleges sent us."

I wrestled with the fear some more so I wouldn't say, "Good. I hope you guys choked so you'll stay home." Instead I said, "You guys are brains. You'll get into college. And then I'll be left all alone."

"I thought you couldn't stand us. I thought you'd be psyched if we left."

I was caught. It wasn't like I could say, "Oh, don't be mental," and admit he was right. I mean, I had always hated it that they were so over-protective. But, after the shooting, it all seemed so different. The papa hawk thing didn't seem to be so bad. Now I couldn't imagine even wanting to step out of the house without major protection. I said nothing. Jesse scanned my face, then he looked at my arm.

"You really have no idea who shot you, do you?" he asked.

I shook my head. "Not clue one."

"We're going to find out who shot you, I promise you that," Jesse muttered, narrowing his eyes at me. His jaw tightened in a way that gave me the shivers. "And when we do . . ." He smacked his fist into his other hand. "I cornered that little jerk Danny the other day and told him if I found out it was him, he'd better be very afraid."

I blinked. "Do you think it was him?" I asked.

Jesse took another shot with the basketball. "Dunno," he said. "A little scag like that . . . Those kinds of guys think they can solve everything by fighting and intimidating people. But they're still scared little losers. We'll find out one way or another."

Jesse left my room, leaving me to wonder why his revenge talk didn't make me feel better. If anything, now I was more afraid than ever. And I didn't know if I was more afraid he'd find the guy who pulled the trigger or that no one ever would.

Over the next few days, with nothing to do but lie in bed and think, I found myself sliding into massive depression. My parents asked me if I would see a counselor, but I cried and told them I didn't want to. They kept trying to cheer me up. Dad and I would play one-armed chess. My mom would read some of my favorite books from when I was little. I know it sounds weird, but it soothed me. Once in a while, my friends called and dropped in after school. The kids in my English class signed this giant computer "Get Well" banner, which my mom hung on the wall by my bed. But anytime it got quiet, I'd start to feel myself go into a moody spiral. And it was at night that I really got scared. When I finally got to sleep, I'd wake up in a sweat, imagining that someone was outside my window with a gun in his hand. I'd imagine him slipping into my window.

"Who are you?" I'd yell, but there'd be no answer. I could see the blinding flash and feel the searing pain. My arm would go into throb overdrive, and I'd scream out into the night.

One morning after I'd awakened several times during the night, my mom told me that something had to be done, that I couldn't put off getting counseling. I rolled my eyes as usual, but later when I got up to go to the bathroom, I don't know why, but I went into this panic overdrive, and I couldn't breathe. My mom found me collapsed in a heap on the floor and she told me she was calling someone *now*. So I nodded. Anything, I figured, had to be better than waiting for that fear to grab me again. So, the next day, this kind of youngish lady wearing a broomstick skirt and a bunch of silver beads shaped like animals came over. She said her name was Theresa, and we talked for a long time. We didn't talk about what happened, but somehow, I did feel better afterward.

Theresa came over again the next day, and she asked me if I was up for taking a walk.

She said we could even walk around the backyard. I thought that would be okay. Even though our backyard was surrounded by high walls, I felt scared. And I told Theresa about being afraid all the time and how sometimes it got so bad that I couldn't breathe. She taught me some deep-breathing exercises and told me I probably had post-traumatic stress syndrome. She said that lots of people get it after really horrible things happen to them. She said we'd do some art therapy and exercises over the next few weeks to help me deal with everything. I slept for a long time after that. It was kind of like I gave my fear over to Theresa With the Weird Beads. Let her figure it out. She was a doctor, and I sure didn't know what to do.

The next day, I was bored, bored, bored as usual, so I called into this radio talk show with some guy named Dr. Dave. I told the screener what had happened to me, and she put me through to Dr. Dave right away. Dr. Dave had me tell my story, then he told me a bunch of stuff like Theresa did.

"The shooting was something that happened to you that you couldn't control," Dr. Dave said. "But your emotional recovery is not going to be something that just 'happens' to you. It must be active, and you must be an active participant in getting over the trauma."

After I hung up, I thought about that for a long time. Then I called Caitlin and told her about it. She was more jazzed that I'd been on the radio than anything.

The next morning, I decided I couldn't stand one more minute in my bed. I got up and slowly did a one-armed dress number. I couldn't button any jeans, so I just threw on a pair of sweats.

"Pa-thetic!" I said to myself in the bathroom mirror as I tried to comb my hair.

I was pretty careful not to clonk my arm against anything as I made my way downstairs. The whole effort made me kind of dizzy, so I had to stop and lean against the door by the kitchen for a moment. I stood there for a moment, realizing that it had been about three weeks since I had been in the kitchen. I hadn't been anywhere but the hospital, the backyard, the bathroom, and my room for all that time.

Walking over to the kitchen table, I sat down where a patch of sunlight spilled through the wooden miniblinds. Someone had left the local newspaper sitting there. Automatically, I turned to the sports pages. I read about Hamilton's recent just-barely soccer win over Riverview High in the state quarter-finals. There were a couple of sentences about me and why I wasn't playing and that the team wasn't playing the same without me. Angrily, I shoved the sports section away and grabbed the front section. Around page three, I saw a small article written about the shooting. It said that no suspects had been found, that the investigation was still ongoing, that special crisis teams had been sent to the school, and that I was recovering. It ended by saying that an emergency parent-teacher meeting was going to be held tonight to discuss "the growing incidence of guns on campus." On the facing page, there was one of those national round-up columns that included a paragraph on a couple of kids arrested in the Midwest for bringing a gun to their elementary school. And below that was another article about some man in Florida who'd shot his wife and two kids. I closed the paper and put my head down on the cool surface of the kitchen table. The gun thing was everywhere.

I couldn't help it. Over the next few days, I found myself reading every newspaper article and watching every TV news show I could about guns and shootings and killings. It was like I couldn't get enough. With each article I read, I'd get more and more angry. Only there was nowhere for my anger to go.

When I told Theresa about this on her next visit, she pursed her lips and played with her weird beads for a while.

"I just don't get it," I wailed. "I'm a good person. I wouldn't hurt anyone. Why did this happen to me?"

Theresa couldn't tell me why. Instead, she talked to me about how bad things happen to good people. Then she told me that it was cool I was reading up on guns and society, that it was helping me become aware of the impact gun violence had on the world. But as I later told Caitlin on the phone, I was already aware of the impact. Especially when she told me how our soccer team had won that last game. And I wasn't part of it, I thought as I hung up the phone. The team had gone out there and won without me. I wasn't really needed anymore. I could imagine Brooke. She wasn't a show-off, but she probably couldn't help loving being the star. I began to wonder if I'd ever want to go out on the soccer field again anyway. Just the thought of it made me feel all shivery. I'd have to talk to Theresa about that. I shrugged my shoulder just to make my arm throb a little to add to my misery.

The next morning, Mom and I went to the doctor's office. Dr. Chen, our family doctor, examined the cast, then removed it. He poked and prodded and told me that it was healing fine. I looked at the raised, angry red scar trailing down my arm and wanted to barf. Dr. Chen put another cast on it and gave me a gray sling.

"It still hurts a lot," I said, not that I wanted to complain.

Dr. Chen nodded and gave my mom a prescription for more painkillers for me, but told me to try to take the pills only when absolutely necessary. Then he said, "I don't see why you can't go to school in a couple of days."

I froze and darted a glance at my mom. She swallowed, and I could tell she didn't like the idea. But she nodded and gave me one of her we'll-talk-about-it-later looks.

As we got into the car in the parking lot, I began to cry again.

"I know," my mom said softly. "I don't love it either, especially since some monster is still out there. But Dr. Chen is right. Your arm is getting better. The school has stepped up its security, and there just isn't much more to be done. You can't hide at home forever, much as we all feel safer with you here. You have to face it again."

"Great," I said. "I have to go school where someone shot me and let them have another

91

shot at me? Is that it?"

"No," my mom said. "Don't get me wrong. I'm not exactly wild about your going back either, but I've had a number of meetings with Mr. Salazar and the rest of the administration. A lot of things have changed since . . . well." She stopped. "You probably won't recognize the place. Caitlin told you about how the kids can't carry backpacks anymore, except for clear plastic ones. Random locker checks. They're talking about metal detectors."

"Sounds like prison," I muttered.

"I'd feel much better if the guy who fired that gun were in prison," my mom said. "But the police have no leads, and now they seem to be too busy to take my calls. I guess they just can't keep up with the caseloads. They told your father and me that every day that goes by weakens the likelihood they'll catch anyone."

"Great," I said and started to breathe deeply like Theresa taught me to.

"But they also said that it was random, and that it's extremely unlikely anyone would come after you."

I leaned on the armrest and thought about the words "extremely unlikely" for a while. Unlikely, but not impossible. Then we pulled into a fast-food restaurant. I ordered a double cheeseburger and a chocolate shake and munched moodily all the way home.

chapter
seven

IT was raining the morning I went back to school. Jeremy honked the car horn in the driveway, and reluctantly, I got up from the kitchen table. I picked up the clear backpack that my mom had bought and started slowly toward the back door. As I passed a mirrored angel that my mom had hanging on the wall by the door, I stopped for a sec to look at myself. On the outside, I didn't look that much different, except that my face was puffier. But inside, I knew I was different. I was not the same J.T. Jenkins. I no longer felt safe and secure in my athletic, can't-touch-me bubble. I was carrying around a world-class lump of fear and I out-worried Caitlin by a mile. Which meant that there was a whole new girl going to Hamilton High School that day. One who was less sure of herself. One who wanted to scream and hide in her room.

Instead, I took a shaky breath and set out for my brothers' beat-up car.

"If you'd taken any longer, I'd have left without you," Jeremy growled as I crawled in next to him.

I smooshed up my face at him to let him know what I thought of him, but secretly I was pleased. He was acting normal and that was all right with me. Jesse squeezed in on the other side. I felt safe between my brothers. Just as we pulled out of our driveway, I saw Caitlin. She smiled that doofy smile she reserved for my brothers and waved. Then she came running over. Without even waiting to be asked, she flung open the back door and slid in.

"Hi, everybody," she said.

Jesse semi-grunted and Jeremy turned on the radio. I turned around as much as I could.

"Hi," I said, taking in her face like I hadn't seen it in a while. Her clear backpack lay on the seat next to her. She saw me looking at it.

"Aren't these plastic things stupid?" she asked. "I mean you can see everything in it. I mean *everything*."

"That's the idea," Jesse said.

"By the way, Tina was asking about you the other day," Caitlin said.

It took me a moment to remember who Tina was. I really hadn't thought about her since the shooting.

"Oh," I said. And I wondered why she should ask about me. I mean after all, she was just someone I talked to in class because there was no one else to talk to.

"So is it weird going back to school?" Caitlin asked, bouncing along to the next subject.

I was ready to say, "No biggie." That's what the old J.T. would have said. I thought about how Theresa had told me that sometimes I'd be tempted to withdraw from people and not tell them what I thought. The new J.T. said, "What do *you* think?"

Caitlin whispered, "I think you can't wait to see Chase."

Yeah, I thought. *I can't wait to see Chase.* The thing was, I wondered what he'd think of the new J.T. I wondered if it showed and maybe I just didn't see it.

As we turned into the senior parking lot and I saw our school marquee with the lettering "SAFE SCHOOLS ARE EVERY-ONE'S BUSINESS," my heart began pounding. I glanced at my sling and fought an urge to scrunch down in the seat. It was like the car was my last safety hatch, and now I was stepping out into scary territory. My high school, which once had seemed like a second home, was now a giant fearscape. I tried not to let it show, but Jesse knew.

"I'll walk you to class," he said.

I smooshed up my face at him to let him know I didn't need him, but he shrugged. He knew I didn't mean it. So with Jesse on one side, and Caitlin on the other side, I breathed deeply and made my way toward first period. I could feel my forehead break out in a sweat as I tried to maneuver down the hall without thwocking my arm against people. I hunched it forward, kind of letting Jesse run interference for me.

"Hey, look at that," Caitlin said, pointing toward the second story by the library.

My eyes followed to where she was pointing to a banner someone had hung that said, "Welcome back, J.T."

"Cool, huh?" Caitlin said.

I couldn't answer. My eyes blurred and this golf-ball sized lump started welling up in my throat. I couldn't believe it. I was about to cry again and I didn't even know why. I must have said "hi" to a zillion people as we walked toward my class. I began to notice how everyone was staring at my sling. It was thick material, but even so, it was as if everyone had x-ray eyes and they were burning a hole in my arm. Unconsciously, I put my hand over it, resting lightly on the sling so that it didn't set off the pain bells again.

What's everyone looking at? I wanted to scream. *Haven't you ever seen a gunshot victim before?* But I didn't scream. I swallowed the lump and smiled because I didn't know what else to do.

Finally, we ended up at the door of my math class. Caitlin took off just as Mr. Hennessey came over. "Welcome back, Julia," he said.

I couldn't believe it. I didn't think he knew who I was other than to tell me to be quiet. Then he stared at my arm until he saw that I saw that he was staring.

Jesse jerked his chin at me and told me to find him if I needed anything. As he disappeared down the crowded hallway, I stuffed down an urge to run after him. Walking into my classroom, I got this weird feeling. I mean, what if the person who'd done this to me was sitting in there? I looked around the room and, wiping my forehead, I wished I could sit in the back of the classroom so no one would sit behind me. I took my seat, but at every sound, I found myself glancing over my shoulder to see what was going on. People started filing into class. They all seemed to look at me, but no one really said anything. It was way too quiet, nothing like I'd remembered our algebra class being before. I think Mr. Hennessey was shocked. When the bell rang, he kind of blinked and told us to open our books.

We were just getting into some equations that I was having trouble understanding when Tina walked into the room. She mumbled something to Mr. Hennessey about her dad's car not starting and plopped her books down noisily next to me. As Mr. Hennessey talked, I stole a look at Tina. Her hair was dyed black, but now it had a blue sheen to it. It made her skin look kind of deathly. She must have felt me looking at her because she turned to give me a cold, blank stare, then turned away. It was weird. I mean, before I was gone, she'd been kind of hanging around me, to the point where Caitlin had been getting all weirded out. Now, it was as if Tina was saying, "Drop dead." Which, when I stopped to think about it, I almost had. Whatever. I tried to force my thoughts back on what Mr. Hennessey was saying. I just wanted things to get back to normal so I could get on with my life again.

During that class, I got a summons from

the guidance counselor's office. I didn't feel like going to talk with anyone, so I crumpled it up and hoped no one would notice. If anyone did, no one said anything. Then, during my biology class, I got a summons from Mr. Salazar's office. Once again, I could feel everyone's eyes on my arm as I walked up to collect the pink slip from Mrs. Pennell. Now what could this be about? My mom had already gone in to talk to him several times over the past few weeks, and he'd already signed my clearance slip. I knew because my mom had shown it to me the other day. And he wasn't going to ask me any more questions about the shooting. I mean, I didn't know anything, and I'd already told the police what I didn't know. This summons didn't make sense.

Slowly, I made my way down the hallway, feeling my heart pound and my breath speed up. Just as I neared the nurse's office, I heard a loud clang. I must have jumped into the air at least a couple of feet high, and I spun around, but it was just a maintenance person who was tossing something into a trash can. The movement had sent off the pain bells again, and I leaned against a door frame for a couple of minutes as I tried to make my breathing normal before walking again.

Opening the door to the principal's office, I tried to breathe the way Theresa had taught me. Slow, steady, even cleansing breaths. "Let the fear leave your body as you exhale," I told myself like Theresa had told me. It was stupid to feel this afraid walking down the hallway at school. No doubt about it, the new J.T. was this total wimp-o-rama.

I handed my slip to the girl working at the desk. Her eyes slid over me in a slippery way after she glanced at the summons. "Wait there," she said in a bored voice and jerked her head in the general direction of a long wooden bench. At least the bench was against the wall, so I didn't have to guard my back.

I sat and watched the hands on the clock. A couple of students came in, and after handing notes to the girl at the desk, squished onto the bench next to me. They looked at me with narrowed eyes, and I could read what they were thinking: "There's the girl who got shot." My arm started throbbing under their stares. I wished Mr. Salazar would call me in and get this over with.

Finally, he appeared around the door. "Miss Jenkins," he said, motioning me to come. I followed him into his office. As I sat facing him at his big desk piled high with papers, he smiled this huge, weird smile that kind of oozed across his face. It was strange. I mean, I'd never really thought much about Mr. Salazar, but now I found that he made me uncomfortable. I shifted around in my chair.

"I'm glad to see that you're feeling better and are able to come back to school," he said, leaning forward.

"Thanks," I said automatically. "I'm glad to be back."

"Did you see the banner that the pep club made for you?"

I nodded. I still didn't get it. From what I knew of the principal, he didn't seem like the type to make small talk. My arm throbbed some more, and I put my hand over it. Mr. Salazar's eyes followed my hand. He cleared his throat.

"I'll get to the point, Miss Jenkins," he said. "I've talked with the police, and it seems they still don't have anything on your case, do they?"

I shook my head. "Not as far as I know. I wish they did. I'd sure like to know what happened—and why."

"So you honestly have no idea, do you?" Mr. Salazar went on. "You know, you can always go talk it over with the counselors we've set up here."

"Uh-huh," I said automatically. "But I don't

know anything."

"You don't hang out with any troubled kids," Mr. Salazar said. It was a statement, not a question. Everyone knew I hung out with the jocks. This was a waste of time. I wished I was back in class.

Mr. Salazar sat back with his hands facing each other, fingertips all touching. "What it gets down to is that we really don't know that it was anyone from Hamilton High at all," he said.

"No," I said, slowly. I hadn't really thought about that. "But we don't know that it *wasn't* someone from here, either."

Mr. Salazar sat up and he looked steadily at me. "Hamilton is a safe school," he said. "We don't have the kinds of problems other schools have."

What was he talking about? I thought back to the day when we'd had the locker search and it seemed that half the police force was on campus. And I thought about the kids hanging around campus sitting on cars and looking for trouble. If he didn't think there were any problems at Hamilton, why the clear backpacks and the talk of metal detectors?

"What happened to you was random," he went on. "It was probably someone from across town."

I blinked. If it was someone from across town, why did everyone think it was Danny? I didn't ask that question, though. I mean, you should have seen the way Mr. Salazar looked at me, like he was daring me to blame a Hamilton student. And, anyway, what could I say? I didn't have a clue. The principal talked on and on about how safe the school really was, and I sat there becoming more and more aware of my arm, which was throbbing like crazy. Then I felt my chest get all tight and I started having trouble breathing. I wondered if I could stop at the nurse's office and take one of my pain pills before going back to class.

When Mr. Salazar finally excused me, I stopped in the nurse's office and took my pill, taking long swallows of water. Ms. Mukai, the nurse, peered at me through her glasses and asked me if I wanted to lie down. By now, my head was pounding. I thought maybe I did. My thoughts were spinning as I lay down on the cot. Why had Mr. Salazar summoned me just to lecture me on how safe Hamilton was? If it was so safe, I wouldn't be lying here clutching my arm.

It was while I was lying on the cot that it occurred to me—I must have done *something* to make this happen to me. It was just too overwhelming to think a person could get shot for no reason. It made me feel so out of control. But as much as I tried, I couldn't imagine *what* it was that I did that caused me to get shot.

Finally, I felt better enough to go to class. I went to my next class and only had enough time to copy down the homework assignment before the bell rang. I gathered up my books slowly and started down the hall. Just as I neared my locker, I saw Chase. He was wearing this cool, blue plaid flannel shirt. His hair had gotten longer, I noticed. It kind of curled under his ear. My heart started thumping wildly as he walked toward me.

"Hi," he said.

"Hi," I said. I just wanted to stand there and drink him in. It had been weeks since I'd seen him, and I'd had plenty of time to think about him during those weeks.

"How's the arm?" he asked.

Pain-free right now, thanks to the miracles of modern medicine, I wanted to say. "Fine," I said, breathing in the smell of the lime after-shave he was wearing.

"I've missed seeing you around," Chase said.

"You have?" I blurted. Then realizing how incredibly lame that sounded, I said, "I've missed being around here, too."

"Well, I'll see ya around," he said. And with that, he was gone.

I leaned against my locker after opening it, waiting for my thoughts to sort themselves out. Wow. Chase had missed seeing me around, I told myself. I wondered exactly what that meant. Whatever. It seemed pretty good. Smiling, I closed my locker and turned around. There, directly in front of me, looking right at me was Danny. His steely look penetrated me, totally blasting the warm, fuzzy feeling Chase had left me with. In its place was an icy fear.

chapter

eight

"YOU are way wrong, Mr. Salazar," I said under my breath. It wasn't anyone from across town. It was Danny. Everyone had been right. It had just taken me a while longer to figure it out for myself. There was no mistaking that look.

I didn't wait to see if Danny was going to try to shoot me again. I took off down the hall so fast. If I thought people had stared at me before, it was nothing compared to the way they stared at me now. I didn't slow down until I got to my social studies class. I ducked inside the door and collapsed in my seat. Ms. Sturges's lesson on Eastern Europe barely registered in my brain. I was too busy trying to shake off that look Danny gave me and wondering what I'd do the next time I saw him. Was I just going to keep running away from him forever? That was just the first question that whirled around in my head. There were a zillion others, like: Why did he shoot me? Had I done something to him and didn't know it? Would he do it again? What would stop him from shooting me or someone else again? Should I do something about my suspicions? Whom should I tell? I mean, the police had probably interviewed him a zillion times. At the end of social studies, I didn't have any answers.

"You okay?" Caitlin asked me at lunch.

"Yeah. Yeah," I said, taking a bite of my sandwich. I could see everyone at our table giving me the eye, but I didn't care. I was getting used to it. I was glad no one asked me about the shooting. I didn't want to burn everyone out by talking about how miserable I was.

Caitlin turned to Alysha sitting next to her and the two of them started talking about something that I didn't pay attention to. Every so often, Caitlin would say, "Right, J.T.?"

I'd nod and pretend that I was listening. But I probably didn't fool anyone, especially when someone knocked over a metal trash can right outside the cafeteria door. My first thought was, "Danny!" My heart shot about a gallon of adrenaline through me so that I jumped up out of my seat and knocked it over backward. I felt my face heat up as I realized everyone was looking at me.

"You okay?" Caitlin asked again.

I smiled lamely. "What a dork I am."

Caitlin patted my good shoulder. "Everyone understands."

"You coming to soccer practice today?" Mia asked.

Brooke glared at her. "She can't play. Of course, she's not," she said.

"Yeah, I am," I said, bristling.

"Yes, she is," Caitlin said loyally.

After my last class, I headed for the girls' locker room, wondering why as I walked. I mean, Brooke was right—I couldn't play. I'd just be a useless blob. But I went anyway just because I didn't know what else to do. I'd come out to this field almost every afternoon since school had begun. Walking into the locker room, I stopped and looked around.

"Still smells the same in here," I mumbled as I was greeted by the stale smell of athletic shoes and moldy towels. A couple of girls eyeballed me, but no one said anything. Caitlin and Brooke and Mia showed up just then, and people started talking again.

Out of habit, I went to my locker and spun the tumbler. It took a while for my combination to come back to me. I felt kind of stupid after I opened my locker, so I let it slam shut.

As everyone suited up and laughed and talked, I went over and sat on the high stool where the towel monitor dispensed the towels after practice.

I watched Ms. Crownover talking on the phone in her glassed-in office. She gave me a thumbs-up sign, and that made me feel better somehow. After a few minutes, she came over to me.

"I'm glad you're here. I could really use your help."

Cool, I thought. *She'll ask me to help coach or something.*

She nodded over to the net bag full of soccer balls. "Can you carry those out to the field?"

"Sure," I said brightly. I tried not to let it show, but I was pretty upset. I'd gone from being a star forward to ball girl just like that. I dragged the net bag out toward the field with my good arm. But then, I felt the familiar tightening in my chest again, and I knew that there was no way I could set foot on that soccer field. I froze.

"Breathe in, breathe out," I commanded myself. I wanted to turn and run, but instead I stood there making myself breathe, and when a couple of girls walked past me, I kind of stepped outside of my body and sort of watched myself move forward toward the field. As I set the bag down by the bench, I looked around the field until my eyes rested on The Spot. I could feel my breath quicken.

Right there. Right in front of the goal. I turned away, but something made me look. Then, in spite of not being able to breathe, I couldn't resist walking over to the spot. I wasn't sure what I expected to see, but all the same, I was surprised. The spot didn't look different than anywhere else on the field. Your basic dirt and grass. No indentations to show where I'd fallen. No bullet marks. No bloodstains.

Turning away, I saw that Caitlin and Mia were watching me from across the field. I shrugged. There was nothing to say.

When everyone got onto the field, I wandered over to the bench and sat down to watch practice. But I didn't sit still for long. It totally freaked me that my back was facing the street, the same street that someone had driven down just a few weeks ago and . . . I shook my head and tried to remember what Theresa had said. Or was it Dr. Dave? Well, anyway, someone said it: Recovery is a deliberate act. It probably wasn't a good recovery strategy to think about the car that hurtled down the road that day. But I couldn't help it. Every so often, I'd hear a car that sounded louder than the others, and I'd spin around to watch it go by. I thought back to that day. It had been crowded on the sidelines. It seemed that almost everyone at Hamilton had turned out for that game. Whoever took a shot out of the car might have been aiming at someone standing on the sidelines. He didn't mean to get me at all. But he did get me.

I shook my head and turned back to watch what was going on on the field. It didn't take long for me to see that things had changed a great deal.

"What have they done to the offense?" I said aloud. Mia had been moved up from midfield to my forward position. A girl named Heather Falchiere had been brought up from the bench to take Mia's place. I'd always kind of written her off because she was a benchwarmer, but actually, I was surprised to see that she had improved a ton since the beginning of the year. She moved the ball upfield and passed it to Caitlin several times, who missed several great opportunities. Ms. Crownover looked cranky and she kept looking over at me. I shrugged.

"My legs are fine. I could kick it in the goal for you," I almost yelled, and I glared at my arm. I felt the crying thing come on again, but

I gulped the tears back in and watched the road as another loud car came screaming down the boulevard.

Finally, practice was over and my eyes followed as my teammates headed toward the locker room. I glanced at the road again, then turned to trail behind my friends, dragging my net bag of balls.

Theresa came over that afternoon and asked about my day. I talked and talked. She had me draw some things in this little sand tray she'd brought. I drew the soccer field and showed her the new plays. She said she was surprised and pleased that I had been able to step onto the field. That made me feel good somehow. We talked about the world being chaotic sometimes and about how people couldn't control everything in their lives. *Tell me about it,* I thought after Theresa left.

That night at dinner, my mom and dad asked me how the day had gone.

"Fine," I said in what I hoped was a perky enough voice for them. I didn't really want to get into it. I'd already told Theresa everything. I wolfed down two loads of mashed potatoes and took a second helping of meatloaf. Comfort food. Whatever. It tasted good.

"They put up a banner for J.T. at school," Jesse said.

"It was huge," Jeremy added.

My mom smiled. "That must have made you feel welcome," she said.

I nodded. Then there was this huge pause.

"Mr. Salazar called me in," I volunteered because my parents were looking for me to tell them something.

My dad's eyes searched my face.

"What did he have to say?"

"He told me that Hamilton was a safe school, and that no Hamilton student could possibly have shot me," I said.

My mom and dad looked at each other with one of those looks I wasn't supposed to see.

"What does he know?" Jeremy exploded, getting all red in the face.

"Chill," Jesse said.

"Whoa, big bro," I said. Jeremy's reaction kind of scared me. I mean, Mr. Salazar's comment was way out there, but Jer didn't have to go all ballistic over it.

"That was very political of Mr. Salazar," my mother said in a cold voice.

I didn't know what she meant, but I wished I hadn't brought it up.

"Please pass the gravy," I said loudly, hoping to change the subject.

After the dishes were cleared, my dad disappeared, then came back into the kitchen.

He thumped my brother's yearbook from the year before down onto the table.

"Let's go through this and see if anything strikes your memory," he said.

"Da—ad," I whined.

"You just never know," Dad said impatiently pushing the book toward me.

"We've already done this," I protested. "I've told you a zillion times that I didn't see anybody. Anyway, this doesn't have anyone in the freshman class in it. Anyway, Mr. Salazar says it couldn't possibly be a Hamilton student."

"Forget Mr. Salazar!" my dad thundered.

I didn't think that Mr. Salazar's bizarreness was that big a deal, but I didn't say so. You don't mess with my dad when he gets that way. So I glanced through the yearbook and—big surprise—no face jumped out at me saying, "I'm the shooter!"

"Dad's getting a little weirded out about this," I whispered to Jesse once Dad had left the room with the yearbook. I didn't add that maybe Dad and Mom should talk with Theresa about how people couldn't control everything in their lives.

Jesse got up and poured a giant-sized glass of milk. "Yeah," he said. "It's got Dad totally wild that no one has a clue."

"I do have a clue," I said, wondering if I

should tell him.

Jesse took a gulp of his milk and wiped the mustache with the back of his hand.

"I guess it's no surprise to anyone," I said. "I think it was Danny."

Jesse's eyes sort of frosted over. "Are you sure? How do you know?"

I shrugged and tried to crowd the memory of Danny's look out of my mind. I tried not to think of how Tina talked about how he knew where to hide guns. "I just know."

Jesse gulped down the rest of his milk silently, and he left the kitchen.

I wandered up to my room and turned on my CD player, then climbed onto my bed and started to tackle my homework. I stopped every so often and wondered if maybe I should have kept my mouth shut. No telling what my brothers might do. One half of me didn't care. So what if they landed Danny a punch or two? But the other half did care. What was to stop my brothers from doing more than landing Danny a couple of punches? Or what if Danny hurt my brothers? And what if I was wrong?

The next morning, I woke up and decided to tell Jesse to forget it about what I'd said about Danny.

After I dressed and did the one-armed hairstyle disaster, I headed downstairs and

116

cornered my brothers hunched over their Fruit Bombs.

"Jesse, about what I said last night about Danny," I said, "Forget about it. I really don't know. I'm probably wrong."

Jeremy looked at Jesse. "Sure, okay," he said.

I wasn't exactly convinced that they got it, but my mom came in just then with her laptop computer, so I shut up.

"Good morning, everyone," she said cheerily.

I didn't see what there was to be so cheery about. It was raining again, like it did practically every day in Oregon. I wondered how it would be to live somewhere else where it was sunny. Somewhere where people didn't go around shooting each other so you didn't have to worry about your brothers getting revenge on them and maybe getting revenge on the wrong person.

I couldn't talk to my brothers in the car about it because Caitlin was there. I'd have to find them around campus as soon as I could.

You know how it is when you're hoping to avoid them and everywhere you turn, your brothers are there in your face bugging you? Well, now that I was looking for them, I couldn't find them anywhere. Finally, I went to Jesse's American lit class, but he wasn't there yet. Glancing at my watch, I saw that I'd have to totally book if I was going to make it to my own class on time.

I shot out of the English wing and started past the maintenance shed to go on to my social studies class. Suddenly, in the shadows, I saw Tina. She stepped out right in my path. She looked as surprised to see me as I was to see her.

"Hey," she said, eyeing me.

"Hey," I said, stepping back from the force of her glare.

"What are you doing here?" she asked, slipping something into the waistband of her pants. She pulled her dark jacket over it.

What *was* I doing here? I didn't know. What was Tina doing here? She smelled like smoke, and all of a sudden I wished I were out of there in a hurry. It would be my luck for some teacher to appear on the scene and decide we'd both been smoking.

"See ya around," I mumbled, then tore out of there.

Halfway to my social studies class, I was suddenly was overpowered by a feeling so strong, it made my knees weak. I'd seen a silver handle in a flash before Tina had flipped her jacket over. By the time I got to social studies, I couldn't even think straight.

Great, I thought. *I'm going totally weird. I'm probably so far gone even Theresa can't help me.*

chapter nine

THE weird feeling stayed with me all day. I was so out of it in my classes, I'm surprised no one seemed to notice. I kept waiting for a chance to talk with Caitlin, but we were constantly surrounded by people. There was a buzz in the air about rolling bones. Rolling bones. Those words again. I'd never gotten around to figuring out what that meant. But somehow it seemed connected to a strange tension crackling through the air on campus.

I managed to snag Caitlin before soccer practice.

"I've gotta talk to you," I said.

"Well, then talk," she replied.

"Not here."

"Fine. We'll go to my house after practice."

"I've got another question for you. Don't laugh. What's 'rolling bones'?"

Caitlin shook her head. "Shooting dice. What's that have to do with anything?"

"Nothing. C'mon, Ms. Crownover will have a cow if you're late getting onto the field."

I sat with my net bag on the bench and scanned the road while my thoughts went wild. Had I seen what I'd thought I'd seen? Was my imagination kicking into overdrive? Was this part of the post-traumatic stress syndrome Theresa talked about it? Could it cause people to think they were seeing guns when they weren't? I turned to watch Brooke stop a ball and send up a shower of mud with her kick while my thoughts chased each other around. I thought about kids shooting dice and gambling and fighting about it all. I thought about scared little people who believed that carrying guns gave them power. I thought about Tina and wondered what she had to do with any of it. Finally, I realized that I couldn't talk with Caitlin about Tina because I really hadn't seen anything. If I told her, she'd probably tell someone else and the whole thing would get out of control. I'd have to have proof before I could accuse Tina of anything.

After practice, I was surprised to see that my brothers weren't waiting for us in the parking lot. I looked at Caitlin and was even more surprised to see that she didn't look disappointed.

"No biggie, we'll just walk to my house, and you can tell me what you wanted to talk about," she said, shrugging and adjusting her plastic backpack over her shoulders.

I hung mine in its usual position over my one good shoulder and we started walking.

"So what's this all about?" Caitlin asked.

I found I couldn't get into it right away, so I babbled about soccer practice until we got to her house. When I stepped inside, I realized that I hadn't been there in ages. Of course, nothing had changed. It was still the cozy mess that I always remembered. It was a mess because Caitlin's mom ran a daycare center out of their house and there were usually a zillion screaming kids everywhere, not to mention toys spilled all over the place. A person had to be in the mood to go over there. Today I was in the mood. It was alive with people and that's where I wanted to be.

When we stepped into the back room, three or four kids looked up from a foam puzzle they were playing with. "J.T.! You came back!" A little girl named Amelia came running over to me. She always did that. As usual, she immediately attached herself to my leg.

"No, Amelia," Caitlin cried, setting down her

bookbag and running over to try to stop her.

"Be careful, 'Melia," Mrs. Holmes said, prying the little girl gently from me. "J.T.'s probably not feeling up to an Amelia attack today."

"I want an airplane ride," Amelia demanded, her hands on her hips. It was something she'd come to expect of me. But there was no way today. My arm had come a long way, but not that far. I wondered if I'd ever be able to pick up the little girl the way I used to.

"I can't," I said, trying not to meet her blue eyes.

Amelia looked up at me and wrinkled her nose. "Why? Are you sick?"

I laughed. "No, I'm not sick." But I didn't explain. How do you tell a little four-year-old girl that you couldn't give airplane rides because someone had planted a bullet and basically totaled your arm?

"See ya later, Amelia," Caitlin said briskly as she almost pushed me toward the kitchen door.

In the kitchen, I dropped my backpack and plopped myself down at the Holmes's scarred farmhouse kitchen table. Moodily, I used my finger to trace over a line that ran partway across the table. "We're talking loser here," I muttered as Caitlin set some of her mom's lemon bars and a carton of milk in front of me.

"Who? Amelia?" she asked.

"No, me," I said quickly. "I'm now the Hamilton soccer team's official ball girl and I can't even toss Amelia around like I used to."

Caitlin pressed her lips together. "Oh, come on, J.T.," she said. "You know it's not like that."

I pushed up my sleeve and checked out my cast. Caitlin looked at it.

"That is why I can't play in the state tournament," I said. "Weird to think that a little thick line of skin is all that's holding me back. Well, that and a bone that probably looks like a road map. You know, I heard my mom and dad talking one night about how this arm could end up being shorter than the other. So now I'll probably be deformed, too. "

"Oh, J.T., you're getting better, and even if worst came to worst and one of your arms was longer, you could still play soccer," Caitlin said softly. "Never mind state. We'll probably lose the next game. I'm already making plans for next year. We'll all be playing tournament soccer in the off-season, and this summer we'll go to soccer camp like we always do. And everything will be normal again."

I munched a lemon bar, but didn't answer. Caitlin was probably right—except for the normal part. And I hated to have a great big feel-sorry-for-myself-athon in front of her, but I couldn't help it. Sometimes it all was so depressing. I mean, one minute I'd been fine, and the next, my whole life was messed up. All because someone had decided to pull a trigger.

After that, we went up to Caitlin's room. I've always liked Caitlin's room. It was decorated with a moon-and-stars theme, mostly dark blue with spots of yellow. I used to wish I'd thought of moon and stars first, I liked it so much. But there was no way I could copy her. And when it got right down to it, I wasn't exactly the type to decorate my room.

Anyway, we settled on Caitlin's floor and played a few CDs and talked about Chase, not to mention Jesse and Jeremy (Caitlin's idea). But then Caitlin surprised me. She started talking about someone named Trevor Gunther, someone I didn't know, who was in her math class. I sat up. There was something new in Caitlin's voice.

"Trevor. I don't know him. What does he play?" I asked.

Caitlin blew back her bangs. "He doesn't," she said.

"Doesn't play soccer, right?"

"Doesn't play sports." Caitlin looked away.

"Oh," I said. Another surprise.

"I think he likes me," Caitlin went on.

I thought about this for a minute. "How do you know?"

"Oh, little things. Like he always seems to hang out by the door and goes into the classroom right when I do and stuff. And the other day, he lent me a pencil and he didn't let go for the longest time when I reached for it. You just know."

"How come this is the first time I've heard about him?" I demanded. I mean, best friends shouldn't keep stuff like this from each other.

Caitlin leaned back on her bed with her long legs running up the wall. " 'Cause you've had other stuff on your mind."

I scowled. It hurt to know that I wasn't fun anymore, that people couldn't talk to me about things. I felt the fear again, only this time it was the fear that I'd changed forever, and that nothing would ever be the same again.

"Oh, come on," Caitlin said. "You know what I mean. And the Trevor thing wasn't really a big deal until today when—"

"When what?"

"Let me finish. It didn't mean anything until he kind of asked me to the Winter Formal."

"The Winter F-formal?" I stammered.

Caitlin nodded her head and this big grin exploded all over her face. But then she shrugged.

"So you are going?"

Caitlin chipped at her boysenberry nail polish. "I dunno. Don't you think it's kind of disloyal to your brothers?"

I almost snorted, but then realized it would do a real number on my friendship if I hurt her feelings by reminding her that Jesse and Jeremy never had paid her the slightest drop of attention. I'd have to handle this smoothly. I mean, I didn't know this guy Trevor, and the fact that he didn't play any sports whatsoever was a strike against him. But he sounded like a nice guy and if he got Caitlin's mind once and for all off my brothers, it might be worth it.

"I think you should go with him," I said decisively. "I mean, Jesse and Jeremy have had their chance. Here's this cute girl right under their noses and they blew it."

Caitlin brightened up at that. "Yeah," she said, tossing her head. "I've kind of been under their noses forever."

"You can say that again. They just don't appreciate a great girl when they see one," I went on. "They're totally unclear on the concept."

Caitlin nodded. "Well, I guess then I'd

better move on. I'll tell Trevor tomorrow."

We were talking about what she'd wear when the phone rang. It was my mom, freaking because I'd forgotten to tell her I'd gone over to Caitlin's. I didn't mention that no one had bothered to show up after practice to give me a ride.

A while later, when Jeremy came to pick me up, Caitlin was cool to him. Too bad Jeremy didn't notice. I did feel a little guilty about talking behind my brothers' backs like that, though. That evening, I was also struck by something else: plain, out-there jealousy. Caitlin had gotten asked to the Winter Formal by a guy she'd hardly known, and here I was totally crushing on Chase since the beginning of the year without a sign that he even felt anything other than pity for me. It made me angry. I was fourteen years old, and I was a loser. Not exactly the most comforting thought to hit the pillow with. But that's how I fell asleep.

The next morning, as I climbed into the car with my brothers, I sensed right away that something was up. Jeremy drove quietly, drumming his fingers against the steering wheel. Jesse seemed tense, like someone had charged him with a dusting of electricity. Caitlin didn't seem to notice when she climbed in. I figured she was already off on Trevor thoughts. It was amazing how quickly she could dump my brothers for a non-athlete. I'd have to check him out at school today.

When we got to school, Jesse reached over and patted my good arm. "Everything's going to be all right," he said.

I didn't have a clue what he meant. Maybe he thought I was still weird about going back to school, which, okay, I was a little. Okay, a lot. But on those first days back, he hadn't been so into how I was feeling. Why now?

Jeremy jerked his chin at me, and I took off.

Caitlin and I went to our lockers, where I got a glimpse of Chase, who threw me a smile. Then I got a total up-close and personal with Trevor. Dark, wavy brown hair. Killer green eyes. A crooked smile. Sum total: a babe.

"Definitely cute," I told Caitlin later. Not as cute as Chase, but not bad.

She didn't seem to hear me. She just kind of floated along the ground and smiled her goofy grin then nearly smashed head-on into someone's locker. I shook my head. She'd never have her head in the soccer game if she kept this up.

I went to math and sat down, ready to endure a long siege with Mr. Hennessey. Just as the bell rang, Tina came in. Mr. Hennessey ticked off something in his roll book, but she just slumped in and heaved herself in her chair next to me.

"Hey," I said as we made eye contact.

She pulled back from me like I was a snake or something. I looked again. No, it was more like she was frightened of me. Talk about weird. While Mr. Hennessey started explaining last night's homework on the overhead projector, I studied Tina. I mean, why should she be afraid of me? Was it because I'd seen her at the maintenance shed? I mean, it wasn't a spot where I'd hang out, but why would she be so afraid? Suddenly she turned and hissed, "Stop looking at me."

So I did. Geez. What was her problem? It had to be something more than bad hair. Toward the end of class, I took one more stealth look at her. My eyes traveled down to her notebook, which aside from her dark, angry ink drawings had a heart doodle with the word "Danny" scripted in the center. So Tina was crushing on Danny, huh? *It takes all kinds,* I thought as I copied the homework assignment in my notebook. Caitlin in like with a non-athlete; Tina in like with a guy who shot guns at people for fun. Then I frowned.

No, it wasn't Danny. I'd known all along it

wasn't Danny. Danny was convenient. Your basic bad boy. He was who everyone wanted to believe did it. It was safer that way. You could just blame everything on him and go on thinking, "That took care of that." So if it wasn't Danny, who was it? I groaned. Not on this endless loop again. My eye fell on Tina again, and I froze. All of the sudden that overwhelming feeling I'd had came rushing back. I was instantly back on the soccer field, running and poised to kick a ball. Then, I heard a loud pop and felt the white-hot sting. Suddenly, I was back at the maintenance shed, and I remembered the silver handle, the way Tina had practically jumped out of her skin when she'd seen me. There was no mistake. I was surprised I'd kidded myself this long. It *was* a gun. *It was Tina. Tina had shot me.*

Just then Tina looked back at me and she knew I knew. Her face went white.

I took off when the bell rang and tore over to where Caitlin was just coming out of her class.

"I think I know who did it," I said breathlessly.

"Finally." Caitlin's voice was hushed. "You're ready to admit it's Danny."

I shook my head. "No. It wasn't Danny. It was Tina Pratt," I said.

Caitlin's eyes bored into mine. "Tina Pratt? Why?"

"Why?" I said with bitterness seeping around my words. "Who knows why someone shoots someone? I don't know why!" But I was beginning to think I knew why. That maybe she'd been in the car driving by the game when she thought she saw someone who'd been hassling Danny. The Danny she had a crush on. She'd show Danny how much she cared by hitting his enemy. Quick solution to an ongoing problem. Trouble was, she'd shot me instead. I'd gotten in the way. I shivered and carefully crossed my arms in front of myself protectively.

"No," Caitlin said impatiently. "Why do you think it was Tina?"

"I don't *think* it was Tina," I said. "Somehow I just know."

Caitlin stood up. "Well, if you think it was Tina—I mean, know it was her—you'd better stop your brothers."

"Stop them from what?"

Caitlin looked at me. "They're going to jump Danny." She glanced at her watch. "They've probably already done it."

"What?!"

"What do you mean 'what'? Everyone at school's been talking about it," Caitlin said. "I was sure you knew. I was just about to ask you about it."

"But I don't know anything. When did you find out?"

Caitlin shrugged. "I dunno. I thought everyone knew. Where have you been?"

"I don't know. Why would they do something that incredibly stupid? Come on, help me find Jeremy and Jesse," I pleaded.

"It's not stupid," insisted Caitlin. "If the police didn't catch him, don't you want someone to get him back for what he did to you?"

"No," I said. "Aside from the fact that it wasn't Danny, revenge doesn't settle anything. My arm's still a mess, and anyway, what happens if someone shoots one of my brothers?"

"Oh," said Caitlin. Now she was starting to get it, and now I was beyond scared.

We took off down the hall and started asking everybody about where we could find my brothers.

"Try the maintenance shed," someone said.

I slapped my right hand against my head. "Of course," I said.

I ran so fast across the parking lot, I left Caitlin in the dust. And just as I got to the maintenance shed, I saw my brothers standing there. Just behind them, I could see Danny in the corner, his face looking closed and dark. He stepped back against the wall, looking like a trapped animal.

Jesse saw me and his eyes grew steely. "J.T., what are you doing here? Get outta here. We don't want you mixed up in this."

"In case you hadn't noticed, I am kinda mixed up in it," I said. "And, no, I won't get outta here."

Jeremy stepped forward, legs apart, arms folded across his chest. "You and Caitlin have to leave. Now." He gave me his best Big Brother.

"Jesse, Jeremy, don't do this," I pleaded. "I mean it."

"J.T., for the last time, get lost." Jesse again. "We're getting back at him for what he did to you."

"He didn't do anything to me," I shouted. My head snapped up as I saw that several students were now gathering around. I wondered how long before campus security or the police came. I had to stop this now.

"You're crazy," Jeremy spat. He went over to Danny and grabbed him by the front of his shirt. It was amazing how little and scared Danny looked. Someone who'd once scared me.

I threw myself on Jeremy. My arm screamed with pain. "Stop it. I mean it. It wasn't Danny."

Jeremy released Danny roughly. "Then who was it?"

"What does it matter?" I yelled. "Even if it was him and you pounded him, so what? So he comes after you with a gun next time, or one of his friends does? What's the difference? It's never going to stop."

Jeremy stepped right up to me. "What's your point?"

"There is no point," I shouted. "Even when they catch whoever it was, there'll be someone else out there. You can't protect everyone, and you can't get back at everyone."

No one said anything for a moment. "Let him go," Jesse muttered in disgust.

Jeremy stepped aside and Danny pushed past me through the throng of students. He turned and gave me a strange look, then disappeared among the students.

"What's going on here?" It was a campus security guard.

"Nothing," someone said.

"Then get to class, all of you," the guard said.

People started breaking up, needing no second urging. Just then I saw Caitlin push through the crowd. She ran over and hugged me. I leaned into her jacket and if I hadn't been crying before, now I was a total faucet.

"C'mon, J.T.," Jesse said. "Nothing much was going to happen."

I jerked away from him. I knew they thought they were helping me, but my brothers didn't get it.

Of course, I didn't get it either, I realized as I walked back toward class, my tears still going at it like they'd never stop. I mean, the scariest thing of all was that what I'd said to my brothers was true: There was never going to be an end to this. And if there'd never be an end to it, how was any of the pain that I'd been through going to make sense? None of us would ever feel safe again.

chapter
ten

"WHO'S gonna win?"
"We're gonna win!"

The next afternoon, I was sitting on the Hamilton High bus with the soccer team as we were on our way to Lakeview High for the play-off game that would determine if we'd be in the state finals championship. I was wearing my purple Hamilton jacket, even though it was a zillion degrees in the bus. And, yes, I had the net bag of balls under my legs.

"I don't even know why I'm here," I muttered under my breath. I told myself I wanted to be in my nice, safe room totally checked out so I didn't have to deal with the fact that I'd be sitting here, once again, watching while everyone else played. My arm throbbed as if trying to add an exclamation point to my thoughts.

"Hey, J.T., you okay?" Caitlin asked me, putting her hand on my other arm.

I shrugged it off. "You're always asking me that."

Caitlin didn't say anything. She just sat there kind of swallowing.

"Better than you," I said lightly. "You're turning kind of green, and let me tell you, it looks totally sicko with purple."

"I'm nervous," Caitlin admitted. She pushed back her hair, which was already getting sweaty.

"You'll cream these guys," I said.

Caitlin laughed. "I honestly don't think so. I wish you were playing, then I'd be more sure."

I looked out the bus window at the gray afternoon darting past. *You and me both,* I thought. But I didn't have to say it.

When we arrived at Lakeview High, we were directed over to the visitors' locker room. It smelled the same as our locker room. I listened as my teammates suited up, laughing and trading insults, and never felt so out of it in my life. Even when Brooke announced over the loudspeaker just before the game that my team dedicated the game to me, it was like I wasn't even there.

I ran out onto the field with everyone, but then headed to the bench, where I sat and bounced a soccer ball between my feet.

We didn't have a chance. Lakeview came out

and scored two goals right away. By the second quarter, they'd scored two more. Even Ms. Crownover's halftime speech didn't do a thing. Though the defense didn't let any more goals get past them, our offense couldn't make it happen. I could see my teammates looking at me. I cursed Tina silently and wondered why again, which did no good. There were no answers.

The bus ride was quiet on the way home, unless you counted some of the sounds of crying. Everyone was so stunned. No one had expected we'd have our clocks cleaned so totally.

"Well, girls, there's always next year," Ms. Crownover said.

Caitlin nudged me and made a horrible face. "There's always next year," she whispered, mimicking Ms. Crownover.

Ordinarily, that phrase didn't do anything for me. It was a consolation after you'd been beaten. But somehow today, it cheered me up. Well, why not? We were alive, and I'd learned not to take that for granted. As long as you were alive, there was hope—and hey, it counted for something. I'd be better next year, and most of the team members were underclassmen, so most of us would be returning. We'd all be a little older, a little stronger, and a little wiser. I was on my way to becoming a lot wiser.

By the time we got back to school, I was strangely cheery. I kicked the net bag into the locker room and hugged everyone I could get my hands on and said, "Good game." Then I stepped outside in the cool night air to wait for Caitlin. I watched as my brothers' chug-a-lug pulled into the parking lot. I wondered if it would be weird seeing them after our last encounter. Caitlin and I walked silently over to the car and slid in.

"We lost," Caitlin said as she slammed the door.

"We know," Jesse said.

"They arrested Tina Pratt this afternoon for participating in a drive-by shooting," Jeremy said. "Yours."

"How did they catch her?" Caitlin asked.

"Danny turned her in," Jesse said.

I sat back in the seat as we started out of the school parking lot, waiting to feel relieved. But I didn't feel relief. I felt the bubble of hope I'd felt earlier sort of pop, and in its place, I felt a sadness and an ache. And I knew I'd never really know why, no matter what happened. And even if I did, it would never change anything. We'd still lost the state semi-finals, and I would be carrying around the scars forever, unable to sit still when someone so much as knocked over a trash can.

Caitlin hugged me gently and we cried, each of us for our own reasons.

When I got home, my parents were all over me, demanding to know about Tina. What could I tell them? I really didn't know her. She was just a girl in one of my classes, one who dyed her hair and had a crush on Danny. But then I realized one thing: Danny had covered for her, kind of letting people think it was him. Why would he do that? Just another thing I'd have to wonder about.

"Wait till Mr. Salazar finds out it was one of his precious Hamilton High students after all," Jesse said with a smirk.

"Talk about stupid."

I looked at my brothers. "He's not stupid," I said softly. "He's just like us. He doesn't know what any of this means either. He's just as scared as we are."

"He's supposed to know. He's a principal," Jesse muttered.

"I don't like the things he said to me, but even though he's a principal, he doesn't have all the answers, I guess. No one knows what to do. So they do dumb things instead. But at least they're trying," I said slowly. "Who knows, if they keep trying long enough, maybe someone will figure out how to stop all this craziness."

My mom tilted up my chin with her hand. "Oh, Julia," she said. Then she shook her head.

Everybody was buzzing at school the next day about Tina and asking me all kinds of questions. I side-stepped them all. My head was already to explode with my own questions.

Just after lunch, Chase came up to me. "Hey," he said.

"Hey," I said, clutching my books and feeling my throat go dry.

"I know you've got a lot going on, but I've been wanting to ask you for a while. If you're not doing anything on the eighteenth, will you go to the Winter Formal with me?"

Just like that. I kind of blinked and nodded, and he smiled and squeezed my right shoulder and smiled goofy like Caitlin does when she's in like.

"I'll call you," he said, then he started down the hall, leaving me to watch the back of his jacket.

"Wow," I thought as a new realization hit me. He'd been afraid to ask me. Weird. But then he'd gutzed up and done it.

Which got me to thinking about courage and all kinds of strange stuff. I was still thinking about it when Caitlin and I walked to Jesse's and Jeremy's car after school.

"Caitlin and I are walking home," I said,

opening the door and leaning in.

"No way," Jesse said.

"Yes way," I said, closing the door firmly and yanking Caitlin's arm.

I didn't need the papa hawks circling around me anymore. There was scary stuff out in the world, that was for sure. But one thing I did know was that I was ready to face it again. No more hiding.

About the Author

Karle Dickerson is a former managing editor of a young women's fashion and beauty magazine based in California. Presently, she is a freelance magazine writer and editor and serves on the board for the Youth Center at St. James in South Pasadena, a program that offers activities as an alternative to gangs and violence. She lives with her husband, three children, and far too many animals.

"I first decided to be a writer when I was ten years old and got my first poem published in the local newspaper," Ms. Dickerson says. "I wrote almost every day in a journal from that day on. I still use some of my growing-up situations that I jotted down then for my book ideas and magazine articles."

Ms. Dickerson spends her spare time attending youth sports activities and buying pet food and supplies.